P9-BYU-836

"Mr. Teggs. How good to see you here," said Lacey, stopping before him and allowing him to lift her gloved hand to his lips. Mr. Teggs smiled as he brought his face up, but, finding Lacey flanked by two zealous gentlemen, he cooled himself and the comment he would have liked to make. "You are, as ever, enchanting, Miss Eden."

"Do you hear, Buzzy! He says I am enchanting. You said my dress was cut too low. You said my..."

"Never mind what I said," replied Buzzy irritably, "and dance with me. 'Tis a waltz."

"And a lovely one. I shall dance it with Mr. Teggs!" returned the lady.

"But Lace, I said you were ravishing!" objected Colleymore. "Surely ravishing ranks higher than enchanting."

"No, enchanting has it," she said, her eyes twinkling, and left on Mr. Teggs' arm as the two astonished men looked on....

Other Fawcett Books
by Claudette Williams:

DESERT ROSE . . . ENGLISH MOON

FIRE AND DESIRE

SONG OF SILKIE

CLAUDETTE
WILLIAMS

LACEY

FAWCETT CREST • NEW YORK

A Fawcett Crest Book

Published by Ballantine Books

Copyright © 1979 by Claudette Williams

All rights reserved under International and Pan-American Copyright Conventions. Published in the United States by Ballantine Books, a division of Random House, Inc., New York, and simultaneously in Canada by Random House of Canada Limited, Toronto.

ISBN 0-449-21139-8

All the characters in this book are fictitious, and any resemblance to actual persons living or dead is purely coincidental.

Manufactured in the United States of America

First Fawcett Crest Edition: December 1979
First Ballantine Books Edition: May 1986

Lacey

Chapter One

THE DRAWING ROOM of the Burton town house was established in the very latest fashion. Its furnishings were well appointed, Regency in design and very expensive. However, at the moment, its two occupants were oblivious to its comforts.

Lacey Burton stamped her dainty foot against the dark, plushy Oriental carpet. "You cannot mean it, Daphne! Even you...wouldn't dare make such an announcement against my will!"

Lady Daphne Burton, Lacey's stepmama, put a hand up to pat her elegantly styled golden curls. The subject was beginning to bore her and she sighed indicating as much. "My dear Lacey...you needn't be so melodramatic about this. I rather thought you were attached to Lord Collymore?"

Lacey took a step backward. She felt as though her

stepmother had slapped her. It was too much to take. Yes, she had been attached to Lord Collymore this past summer, desperately so, and then she had grown up quite suddenly on her eighteenth birthday when she had discovered that Daphne and Collymore were lovers! Now as she remembered all the hurt that she had endured, she attempted to control herself. She shook her head of short, chestnut-colored curls, and though her dark eyes glistened with trapped tears, her voice was steady. "I had a schoolgirl crush on him for a time, but that, *ma'am*," she used the word deliberately, "...was before I knew him to be *your* lover!" Ah, a flush hit, she thought victoriously. Good! She never knew until this moment how very much she disliked Daphne.

"That is quite enough!" snapped Lady Burton rounding on Lacey angrily. Her blue eyes were small balls of ice and her mouth was set in a hard line. "Your easy tongue is to be despised!"

"As your easy morals!" retorted Lacey furiously.

Daphne took a step forward but she held herself in control. She wanted desperately to slap the girl's face. Really, it was more than she could bear. The London season was upon them and it was her duty to bring Lacey out. If Lacey's father had been alive, there would have been nothing to it, for she would have had to do the thing. But he was gone now an entire year and she had no intention of taking on a dowager's role! The very notion disgusted her. She was scarcely five and thirty, undeniably lovely of face and figure and totally unequal to the task of chaperon. Moreover, Lacey had metamorphosed into quite a dashing beauty... and it was quite possible that her stepdaughter would steal the scene if she were to allow it. But she wouldn't. No, indeed!

She did a tour of the room and, very much in

control, said quietly, "I shall overlook your rudeness. Lord Collymore is not interested in me. Quite frankly, my independence is nothing to your fortune. Your father did me an injustice in that dratted will of his. However, that does not signify. Collymore has made an offer for you."

"Of course...a marriage of convenience would suit him very well. He is, I understand, in financial difficulty!" said Lacey with much disdain.

"How very well informed you are for a chit just about to be presented to the world. Where, I wonder, do you come by all this worldly information?" said Daphne in great dislike.

"It doesn't matter. Just as long as you understand that I shan't marry him," said Lacey, folding her arms across her trim midriff. "There is no way, ma'am, that you can force me to it."

"Don't you think so, dear? You know little of me, then. I intend to set it about that I found Lord Collymore in a compromising position with you above stairs! Indeed, you will have no choice but to marry him or find yourself ruined! What chance have you among the ton if they thought you despoiled?" It was sweetly said.

Lacey stared with disbelief and her words when they came were scarcely audible. "You are wicked, Daphne. I don't know how Father fancied himself in love with you!" So saying she fled the room to race up the stairs, her white muslin skirts flying about her feet. When she reached her chamber she bolted the door behind her. Her room was made up of creamy satin and lovely flowered paper but its design did little to mollify her agitation. Completely spent, she rushed to her bed and sank into its downy softness.

Lord Collymore wanted her for her inheritance. How despicable! She sighed over this, for it had not been so very long ago when she had found herself in the throes of a deep infatuation with that particular rakehell. No matter. She was over it now. But what was she to do? She must do something. Vanish? She wished she could vanish. If she weren't here, Daphne could not begin her strategy. But where . . . ? And then a light dawned in her eyes. Of course. A small toy poodle that had been asleep on the hearth rug had awakened and padded to her bed, whining. She bent and lifted the fluff of gray into her arms. "Oh, Peewee . . . it must work . . ."

A neat black carriage emblazoned with the owner's coat of arms was swiftly tooled 'round a tricky bend in the road. There was scarcely any moonlight breaking through the heavy sky. Clouds scudded, their texture promising spring showers. The coach's occupant had reason to leave London in haste, quite excellent reasons indeed, and therefore urged his driver onward in spite of the threatening weather.

Sir Roland Keyes had that very day sustained some damaging losses. The elfin woman he had courted all season for her beauty and her fortune had rejected him. Damn, but what a rejection . . . enough to remember for a lifetime. Ruefully he recalled the way in which Myriah had jilted him. He had nearly had her . . . but then Kit Wimborne entered the scene and all was over. To be sure, he had behaved the cad and deserved no better than he received, but that did not diminish the blow or the humiliation. He had left Myriah in the arms of Kit Wimborne . . . and returned to London to find his creditors at his door. Fiend seize their souls, he needed more time. He had managed to stave off some of them with the winnings of a horse that had come in that very morning, but the others...? He'd have to keep them off by absenting himself.

The future? It looked black, he thought sullenly. He would have to court another heiress. A depressing thought, to be sure. Myriah had been different, exciting. He had not been in love with her, but certainly life with her would have been amusing. Her aqua-blue eyes and wayward notions were uplifting. Ah, well, Myriah probably would have proved tiresome in the end and he had the satisfaction of knowing that his heart had not been in it. With his heart very much intact and as hard as ever he made his way up north. Nottingham was his objective, where a certain viscount he had long enjoyed a friendship with would be happy to give him shelter until he could repair his losses. There was too a notable heiress in Nottingham. He would seek her out and perhaps...?

A lone rider, not overly distinguished in appearance and, in fact, bearing the overall impression of a youth, schooled a high-spirited black gelding over the dark North Road. In a straw basket secured to the saddle lay a trusting toy poodle; it whelped as its owner suddenly gave a right lead and scooted off into a controlled canter.

Lacey's instincts had been tickling her for the past fifteen minutes. She was not alone on this road. But who was watching her, following her? She could not tell. She was dressed in boys' breeches and a short buckskin riding jacket. A lad's top hat sat low over her chestnut curls. This disguise was a precaution for the long trip north. At her saddle's back was a neatly packed portmanteau. In her hessian was a fat wad of cash, and at her waist a small ladies' pistol. She fingered it now. It was dangerous whipping up her

11

horse in the dark, for the road was unfamiliar. But someone was watching her—she was certain of it—and this boded ill.

She had not long to concern herself about this, for suddenly, out of the thicket, came two dark riders! Highwaymen! She knew it from the way they came at her, from the slit eyes gleaming behind their masks, from the way they smiled at her—a smile that meant her no good, their yellow teeth exposed. If only she could manage to hide the fact that she was a female....

"Well now, stripling..." bellowed the larger of the two men, "You'll save yerself a stash of trouble by handing over the ready... nicely now, nicely..."

Lacey could have knocked her head into a nearby tree. How stupid of her not to foresee this. She should have prepared some loose cash on her person. If she went into her boot and took out the wad of cash, she would be left without a sou... She stalled for time. If only the stage would come by... if only... "I haven't any money," she said in a low, frightened voice.

The smaller man gave over a harsh laugh, "Haven't you? Well, then, green 'un... off the horse... we'll jest 'ave a look-see..."

"Please, sirs... couldn't you leave me be and go after fatter game?" she pleaded. "I haven't any money... I am running away you see..."

"Running away are ye?" chortled the large man. He studied her a moment and then ran an experienced eye over the horse. At first he thought her nought but a moonling lad, but upon closer inspection a certain knowledge infiltrated his hazy mind. This was a wench! She was running away dressed as an urchin... now that was worth a farthing or two. "Lord love ye... let's 'ave a better look at ye... for I'll be hanged if ye be not a pretty chit!"

"Whats that ye say? A wench?" asked his partner.

"Aye then...a dear wench..." said the other reaching out and catching Lacey by the waist.

"Let me go, swine!" screamed Lacey and the sound of her voice echoed all around. "Let me go!"

Sir Roland's coach had slowed to give its four horses a breathing spell and its owner opened a window for air. Something caught his attention and he rapped his driver to a halt. "What the devil was that, Todd?"

"I dunno, sir." answered the driver lazily. He had heard nothing. He was tired and wanted nothing more than to reach the posting house and get into bed.

Again, Sir Roland heard the unmistakable sound of a female; she was definitely in trouble...and not far down the road. With lightning speed he whipped off his top hat and greatcoat and took hold of his horse pistol. Jumping out of the coach he ordered curtly, "Wait here and be armed, Todd!" and then he vanished into the darkness as he took the road, hugging the woods lining it.

Swiftly, nimbly, he brought himself to the thick of things. What he saw was a brutish highwayman bullying a girl in boy's clothing. There were two highwaymen—one held her arms, the other tore at her riding jacket. Sir Roland raised his pistol and took careful aim. He got off his first shot nicely, making his mark in the arm of the man ripping away at the struggling girl's coat.

The small man jumped away in screeching pain. He looked 'round him but could see nothing. His partner too had relaxed his hold on Lacey to scan his surroundings and then a deep male voice resounded from the thicket.

"You would be wise to put down your weapons and

attempt to escape." Even as Roland got out the last words he had changed his position.

The big oaf holding Lacey released her altogether and aimlessly shot his gun off toward the voice. For his efforts he received an answering shot that left his left arm hanging uselessly at his side. "Gawd! Let's get out of here!" he cried, rushing for his horse.

"Aye..." agreed his cohort.

Sir Roland watched them ride off. It was just as well, he thought. He had no intention of pursuing the devils. Best to see to the girl and be on his way. He stepped out of the woods and into Lacey's full view. The moon's light haloed him—or so it seemed to Lacey—as she watched him come forward. He was tall and elegantly clothed. There was a silver tinge to the temples of his auburn curls. Handsome. It tickled her senses that he was very handsome. But...he looked to be in the latter part of his twenties...near to thirty...and he looked every bit the rake. Careful, she told herself. You have already been stung by just that sort!

Sir Roland's spirits had picked up. He had definitely been fortified by the preceding events. Earlier he had been in control but suffering the storm of quiet raging. He had needed a release and he had found it. He was well disposed to the curly headed, dark-eyed chit in boy's clothing. He came forward, smiling. "I do hope they have not harmed you." His voice held concern.

"Thank you..." returned Lacey going closer to him on a breathless note, extending her gloved hand.

He took it up with interest and noted that it was both delicate and trembling. He gave it a reassuring squeeze before releasing it. Her voice had the tone of quality...yet here she was on the open road, dressed

14

immodestly in male attire...and she was alone. Strange, and most intriguing. "It was my pleasure to assist you, Miss...?"

This was a clear invitation. It would be rude to deny him her name but she didn't want to give it out. What to do? Prevaricate. It was the only solution. She couldn't possibly tell him she was a Burton without bringing Daphne down upon her...or worse, involving the entire family in scandal. "Eden..." she supplied easily, feeling only a slight twinge of guilt, "Lacey Eden."

"Ah, then, Miss Eden, perhaps you will indulge me a moment. What brings you to the North Road at this hour...alone?"

"I...I had no choice," she said, hopelessly trying to think of a plausible explanation. Perhaps in the end a half-truth would serve?

"Didn't you? Well then...now you do," he said suddenly, not sure why he was doing this. "I have a coach not far down the road and I should be delighted to convey you to the nearest posting house."

"But...that would be most...what I mean is...I couldn't possibly accept. It would not be in the least bit proper. I don't even know you," she said in some confusion. Secretly she was quite willing to be convinced to take up his offer.

He let loose an amused chuckle. "But your mode of travel"—he eyed her for emphasis—"is of course above reproach?"

She had the grace to blush darkly, "No...it is not, of course...and you have every right to think what you will of me...but..."

"I know...you had no choice," he provided for her with a winning smile. Really the chit had been through an ordeal with those ruffians. He could think

15

of many a lady who would now be swooning in his arms. She was probably a schoolgirl running away, he decided.

She gave him an answering smile. "I really do appreciate everything you have done but... I must go." She moved toward her horse.

He frowned. He couldn't let her start out alone. It was a fiendish notion. She was so small... so helpless... her dark eyes were too entrancing. "Please, Miss Eden... reconsider. My journey takes me to Nottingham. Couldn't—"

She cut him off short, "Nottingham? Why... that is exactly where I am going!"

"Then"—he smiled victoriously—"you will admit that this was meant to be! Predestined."

"What an intriguing notion."

"Then... you will allow me to escort you, Miss Eden?" He hesitated. "I promise you... you have nothing to fear from me."

"Well, then... oh, I don't know your name!"

"Sir Roland Keyes," he answered quietly.

"Well, then, Sir Roland, I accept your kind offer."

He smiled, well pleased with her decision, and stood back to watch as she took the reins of her horse and tugged him along. This trip might prove to be amusing, after all! he said to himself.

Chapter Two

SIR ROLAND BUSIED himself with lighting the oil lamps on the interior wallboard of the coach and was unaware that a small fluff of gray had peeped its head out of the straw basket at his guest's feet. However, the fluff sniffed the air and disapproved with a small but rather ferocious woof.

Brows up expressivefully, Sir Roland fixed his quizzical gaze upon the curly gray ears noting with some distaste the red ribbons fixed theron. "What is that?" he asked with some repugnance.

"He is my dog, Peewee," answered Lacey brightly: however, the toy poodle had by then discovered a nook in which to relieve himself. Horrified, Lacey watched as her pet did a head spin, raised a leg and nicely christened Sir Roland's coach floor.

"Peewee, you say? Appropriate," returned Sir

Roland caustically. "Tell me ... does it always do that when someone has been foolish enough to offer it shelter?"

Lacey's face flushed deep red. "Oh...I am so sorry...he has been cooped up in the basket for hours...and...oh, my..." She was grabbing for the handkerchief she carried in the inside pocket of her riding jacket, bending to drop it in Peewee's puddle, when she found a strong clasp take hold of her hand.

Sir Roland was controlling a quivering lip, for the entire thing suddenly struck him as ludicrous. "No, child, don't fret yourself." He gently pushed her back into her seat, then he dropped his own large, white handkerchief onto the stained floorboard.

"You naughty boy, Peewee!" reprimanded Lacey, wagging her finger at the crouching thing. He had by now assimilated that he had done the forbidden. "You should have told me you needed a run!"

"You mean it talks as well?" teased Sir Roland.

She looked up sharply and then a warm smile lit up her countenance. "Oh, I see now, 'tis but a hum. You are a right one, after all. I thought so from your eyes." She sighed contentedly. "You are so very understanding. My stepmama would have gone on about it for hours."

He controlled his curving lip. He had never been taken in by so angelic a light before and he refrained from correcting her opinion. However, he was curious now about this new piece of intelligence. "Your stepmama...is that from whom you are running away?"

"In a way...yes," she said. Indeed it came in clearly that a half-truth would do nicely.

"No doubt she comes straight out of some fairy tale. Hoary, old and evil?" bantered Sir Roland, wondering what the deuce he was doing at this hour conversing with a hoyden of a girl.

"Oh, no...she is quite young...well, at least not old. Five and thirty, actually. She is very lovely...but, oh, she has such a wickedly selfish heart." She sighed and then lowered her voice as though someone might be lurking about with eavesdropping on their mind. "Wants me out of the way."

"Does she? Why?" This was fast becoming tantalizing, thought Roland, intrigued in spite of his sophistication. There was such a brightness in the girl's dark eyes. Most captivating, he reflected as he watched her face.

She had gone too far, of course. She bit her lip. What to answer him now? She couldn't tell him why. She had run away with every intention of taking on a new role in life, for a while at least. Marriages of convenience! Bah! She would have no such thing thrust on her. She was practical enough to realize that it would not be comfortable to do without her fortune, but it would be reassuring to know that someone wanted to marry her whether she had one or not! She would invent a nice tale, she decided.

"You see...Stepmama and I have existed this past year on a nippy competence. Quite paltry, really..." She felt the blush steal into her cheeks but continued her story steadfastly. "Wants me married off. An old buzzard made me an offer...wants to pay a handsome settlement. Won't be auctioned off, so I escaped!"

"Very ingenious, but I am not certain it was very wise." Even as he spoke, his thoughts ran to her black gelding. An expensive mount, that one. "You must have had some comforts at home...your gelding, for example, has been well groomed?"

"Cricket? Yes...he was a gift from my father shortly before he died...and our stables keep us in debt. My stepmother lives high, much higher than our means...that is why..."

"...she wants that handsome settlement," he finished. "So, a marriage of convenience?" He was smiling ruefully, for it was just what he planned for himself. "It is not so very wicked to want you well established."

"But I do not want the match! He is... horrible...old...ugly. It is not *my* welfare she has at heart, I do assure you!"

"My dear child..." he started. This was beginning to bore him.

"I am not a child!" she snapped, picking up his interest once again as a warm light glowed in her dark eyes. Quite fascinating, he thought.

With much hauteur, she explained, "I turned eighteen some months ago and would have been brought out this season...had my stepmother any principles!"

"Of course," he said maintaining his gravity. This was really none of his affair but he found himself saying, "She cannot, I am certain...force you into a marriage with someone you dislike."

"Oh, can't she? You don't know her, and what is more...I had friends with perfectly loving parents...who made marriages of convenience, not by choice! Parents are *not* always wise."

"But where will you go?" He was worried about his question. Why should he concern himself? He had his own problems!

"I have already told you, to Nottingham."

"A perfectly amiable town, but how can it serve you better than Stratford, Beresford or any number of lovely towns?" he teased.

She looked up sharply and found the twinkle in his hazel eyes. Such laughing eyes, she thought. "I have a friend in Nottingham. When last I saw him, I considered marrying him," she said matter of factly.

"I see...and this friend of yours in Nottingham...he expects you?"

"Oh, no, there was no time, but that does not signify. We have the closest relationship...always have..."

"Have you taken into account the possibility that you might find yourself in the suds should he prove to be away from home?"

"No. I know that he is there. He has only just left London, you see. His mother, Lady Bussingham, declared that she was all worn out and needed a rest at their country home..."

"Buzzy? Buzzy is your friend...?" he ejaculated incredulously.

"Why...yes...do you know him?"

"Know him?" he said ruefully thinking of all the glory days of his youth spent in this friend's company. "You might say that. In fact, as it happens, I am on my way to join him at Bussingham Towers!"

"Oh, dear," said Lacey over a frown, "that does pose a problem. However will I explain to Lady Bussingham...?"

"Never mind that now. We shall hit upon something. However, I do want to know..." He hesitated lest he offend.

"What?" she urged.

"You said awhile ago that you had considered marrying Buzzy when last you saw him?"

"Y-es?"

"When was it you last saw him?"

"Last week," she said, wondering what this was about and thinking she now had a new problem. She would have to convince Lady Bussingham and her son the viscount to keep her secret. She was preoccupied with this and did not notice his astonishment until he laughed out loud.

"That dog!" he exclaimed. "He never mentioned to me that he was planning on marrying anyone!" He recollected reasons to think quite the opposite but kept this very much to himself.

"Well...he wasn't, you see."

"I don't think I understand."

"Buzzy has never proposed to me. It was only recently that the notion even entered *my* head," she said in way of explanation.

"Good God!" uttered Sir Roland.

She smiled amiably. "I do hope Buzzy shan't take it like that. Now, if you don't mind, sir, I should dearly like to curl up and fall asleep."

"Yes, of course, please do," said Sir Roland at once, and was amazed some moments later to discover that she had done just that.

Sunlight! It hit Lacey's eyes with sweet warmth and she stirred. Her dark lashes fluttered against her white cheeks, opened and then closed. Sunlight! Its meaning dwelt in her mind a moment before she sat bold upright in her bed.

Where? How? She tousled her short chestnut curls with her hands attempting to shake off her sleep. She was in a bed...? Then it all came flooding back to her. She looked down at herself. Her riding coat was gone; her shirt had been loosened at the neck. *He* must have done that! Well, she smiled ruefully to herself, she should be happy he did not remove all her clothing! But really, it was genuinely sweet of him. Such a gentleman. There was nothing lacking in his conduct.

How gently he had carried her out of the coach. She recalled looking up to find his shoulder very near, to find herself cradled in his strong arms. Candlelights...? Men...drinking...? An inn. She had realized that they had arrived at a posting inn. She had stirred, said something into his shoulder. He had pulled her hat low over her eyes.

"Go to sleep little one...and not a word," he said on a hushed note, before taking the stairs. He had already signed for two rooms. He had been careful to identify her as his young brother; he wanted no mishaps now.

She had sighed and snuggled into his embrace. It was so comfortable to allow him to take command...she was too tired to do otherwise. Lacey...how could you? she asked herself now. My word, you have behaved very loosely to say the least! You could be ruined and it would be your own hand that works the trick, not Daphne's!

She stretched in answer to this and made her way to her washbasin, where she refreshed herself. A mirror told her that her chestnut curls were in some disorder. She attempted to set things right by ineptly using her fingers. This proved impossible. Her hair would remain a jumble until a comb and brush could be had. A knock sounded.

She went to the door and opened it at once. He stood there smiling and it flickered across his mind that she was a veritable rough-and-tumble beauty! She on the other hand was struck by the polished sophistication that hung about his handsome head. He had appeared by the light of the moon quite an attractive blade, but her impression then was nothing to what it was now. Such eyes! Gold flecks twinkled in the recesses of his pupils. His hair was a mass of auburn waves interlocked to the neck in perfect disarray, with silver streaks at his temples. How sensually alluring, she thought. She rather liked his shoulders, which were broad and well fitted by his buckskin riding coat. He was a Corinthian, of course. She knew that because Buzzy never neglected pointing out the difference between such notables and the dandies about town. No dandy this man!

"Sir Roland...where is Peewee?" she asked immediately, stepping aside to allow him entry. She should not be letting him into her room. He was a man...a stranger...but she dismissed this consideration the moment it entered her head.

He smiled. "Peewee has been fed, walked and deposited in my coach." He noted the blush in her cheeks, the brightness of her dark eyes, the confusion as she watched him close the door at his back. "Now, I am afraid, my dear, that we shall have to leave at once...and without feeding you—"

"Not feed me?" A horrendous thought considering the state of her internal affairs. "But I am famished. You cannot mean it!" Forgotten was the agitation of finding herself in a bedroom with him. He had set aside blushing fancies with hard-core realities.

He chuckled, "No, no, never fear, little one, I shall feed you, but not here. I have taken a basket of buns and shall have a mug of hot cocoa brought to you in the coach as we pull out..."

"But why?"

"Because while I was able to fob you off as my young brother by the cloak of night, you would not be able to pull off the stunt in broad daylight."

She blushed. "Oh...of course."

"Can you be ready to leave in ten minutes?"

She smiled. "Can you bring me a shirt from my portmanteau? I should like a change of linen?"

"Affirmative minx, but mind now, keep your hat

24

tucked low over your head and the cloak well 'round your shoulders as you descend the stairs. No side trips once there... straight to the coach!"

"Aye, aye, Captain." She laughed happily.

He smiled, not displeased with her attitude. She was a plucky girl this one and he rather admired her. She stalled him at the door.

"Sir Roland...?"

"Yes, Miss Eden?"

"Thank you."

He said nothing. He didn't need to, and then she was left to her thoughts. Her thoughts? Excited. Too turbulent to read, to understand. An adventure was starting. Her first since her childhood and something told her it would be far better than anything that she had experienced then!

Chapter Three

ABSENTLY LACE RAN her hand over her sleeping dog. Peewee, his head nestled upon his front paw, sighed contentedly as the coach rumbled smoothly over the well-used road. For the first time that morning Lacey had fallen silent. She suddenly realized that she knew nothing about the man sitting opposite her. He was watching the passing landscape; she was watching him.

"Tell me something if you will, Sir Roland...?" she said lightly, bringing his attention 'round once more. She was curious about him. She had told him much about herself, discounting the sidestepping of truth; however, he had told her virtually nothing about himself.

"Something? What kind of a something?" he teased. She was a veritable pixie. They had been traveling for some three hours. Her banter was lively, invigorating, bubbling, fascinating in so many ways that he was well pleased to have her as a traveling companion. But while she saw an extremely attractive male possibility, he saw only a child. Adorable, to be sure...but still, only a child.

"About yourself, of course," she answered in some surprise.

"What about myself?" he answered cautiously.

"Well...for instance, why do you go to Nottingham?"

"Why, to visit with my friend Viscount Bussingham," he answered easily, doing some sidestepping himself.

"Yes, of course," she retorted impatiently, "but I find that all very odd."

"Do you? Why?"

"Aha! *You* need not run away! No one is trying to force your hand. It is the height of the season...Almacks...the theater...Vauxhall, why just everything is opening in London to full capacity...yet you are off to Nottingham. Strange."

"Clever minx! I don't suppose I should attempt to pull the wool over your eyes?" His own were lit with amusement. "No, I didn't think so," he said in response to her answering with a vigorous shake of her head. "But I could of course say...'tis none of your...er...affair..."

"How horrid that would be for me. No, you must not say that. Find another way of letting me down," she retorted at once.

He laughed. "What a minx you are. No, I shan't let you down. Why am I going to Nottingham? Well, the sorry truth is that while you go to escape marriage, *I* go to find it."

She felt strangely agitated by this statement. It

was not what she wanted to hear. "Whatever do you mean?"

"I mean that I go as Buzzy's guest to court a lady within the vicinity of Bussingham Towers. She is, if my facts are correct, a very rich young woman."

The pixie face before him was moved into sad shock. "Oh...you cannot mean that you are a fortune hunter? How...perfectly odious."

"I am afraid, though why I should be telling you this, but...never mind, I am telling you that yes, I am indeed a fortune hunter. I was not always so and to be sure, it is not what I like...but the dogs are at my heels Lacey and I am ruler of my fate no more."

"But...what does that mean?"

"It means that I am no different than any other gentleman in narrow straits. There is but one course to follow and that is to marry for convenience. To combine name and title to fortune."

"But...do you mean to play some poor heiress false?"

"No. I rather fancy myself an honorable man in that regard. I have no intention of pretending an attachment for a maid I have never seen."

"Oh, my word...! You mean...you actually mean you have never clapped eyes on this woman in Nottingham? How then can you court her...I mean, it seems all very...uncomfortable to me."

"That—" he flicked her nose with his finger—"is because you are a naïve child," he said gently, and then before she could object, "You see, my minx, marriages of this sort are a common practice among our class...and don't tell me you are not aware of that!"

"Why, yes I am, but..."

"But nothing! There's a wealthy mill owner in Nottingham. It's something of a comedown for a member of my family... but it just so happens that wealth wipes out such considerations. This mill owner has yet another attribute... a daughter of marriageable age. He has presented her in London and she did not take. An odd circumstance considering the size of her portion and one can only shudder at the obvious reason. However, that is neither here nor there... I believe they will accept my suit."

"But... you mightn't like her... and think how ... distasteful that would be."

"I have given that a great deal of thought and happily, if such turns out to be the case, we may make suitable living arrangements," he said on a dry note.

"But... but..."

"Hush now. I have no wish to argue with you about my future. Shall we instead, discuss yours?"

She sighed, "*I am* rather worried... about lunch."

He stared at her a moment and then let out a long laugh. "About lunch you say?"

"Well, you may have considered that bun and cocoa breakfast substantial... but I should not like to repeat much of the same for lunch... You don't mean to keep me in the coach again, for I won't have it!"

"I see a solution must be found if we are to protect your reputation, for you must know, my dear, that if you were seen alone in my company you would have nothing left to shield." He said this on rather a grim note.

Lacey studied him with pure interest. "Oh... never say you are a rakehell?" Her eyes were fiery.

"I am," he said gravely, trying to put a damper on her high spirits.

"How very exciting. I would never have guessed, for you don't seem interested in seducing me," she said amiably.

30

He was taken aback. "I don't, as a matter of course... er... seduce young virgins."

"Ah... but how do you know that I am one?" She was bantering with him, of course, and only slightly aware that this was most improper conduct.

His eyes twinkled, "Vixen! Experience, my girl, experience."

She sighed, "Hmmm. I am quite certain you have that. But now, to the problem at hand. We could pretend you are travelling with your sister. I could be she!"

"So sorry... no sister."

"We could pretend...?"

"No. We might meet some chance acquaintances of mine... wouldn't do," he answered brightly, pleased to have this out of the way.

"What then?"

"You will remain in the coach and I will fetch you all manner of delectables."

"Chocolate tarts?" she bargained.

"Certainly not. Cheese, fruit, bread..."

"And chocolate tarts," she insisted.

"If you promise to eat your meal first," he said on an authorative note.

Her eyes laughed, her cheeks dimpled, "Oh, yes, Papa."

He frowned depressingly, and for some unreasonable fancy the term "papa" jarred his sense of himself. However, there was no time to contemplate this, for they were fast pulling up to the posting house and as he prepared to alight he wagged a finger.

"Keep your hat low over your forehead; keep your cloak well 'round your pretty shoulders and do not get out of the coach!"

"Oh, very well, Sir Roland, though in truth I do

31

think you are making a bit too much out of all this."

He didn't bother to answer because he was already moving across the cobbled courtyard and then her voice called 'round his head.

"Don't forget the chocolate tarts!"

It was evening and its sweet smell wafted through the open window of Lacey's bedroom chambers. They were on the last leg of the journey and as Sir Roland leaned back in his Windsor chair he sighed over this thought with some relief. His hand sought and found in his inner pocket a brightly painted snuffbox. He flipped the lid open with one hand and took a delicate pinch.

Lacey slipped a sweetmeat into her mouth and smiled. "You do that rather well."

He inclined his handsome head. "Thank you. Have you had quite enough dinner? Shall I remove the tray?"

"Hmmm. It was delicious, but you stay there. I'll just put the tray outside the door." Really he was remarkable. Spiriting her up to this room, fetching a dinner tray for her so that no servants could catch a glimpse of her. She sighed with satisfaction, opened the door and bent to leave the tray upon the hardwood floor when something caught her eye. Beautiful. It was the first word that came to mind as she looked at shining ringlets of flaxen gold. Gold? No, softer, whiter, finer. The face ... ? Angelic. Round blue eyes in a round soft face of alabaster. Lovely. These were Lacey's first impressions as she saw the young maid make slow, laborious progress up the wood stairs. Wrong? Yes, something was wrong with the way the girl moved. Her burdensome luggage? Yes, but something else, and then with a wave of pity she realized the beautiful maid was severely handicapped by her left leg. Without thinking she went forward, for the luggage was simply too much for any one woman to carry alone.

"Here...do let me help you..." said Lacey, taking hold of one large portmanteau.

The angelic face smiled, though there was a hint of surprise when she took in Lacey's state of dress. "Oh, no, I can manage...really."

"I am certain you can, but since I am here and fully capable of helping you...why don't you let me?"

"How very kind...thank you," said the girl accepting graciously. "I was told our room is the corner one..."

Sir Roland was by now standing in the doorway watching the two females make their way down the hall. He cursed softly beneath his breath. What to do? Stay out of it? Yes, better not to display his presense and allow any awkwardness to enter the situation. He retreated quietly back into Lacey's room but he was seething with silent irritation.

Lacey put down the large portmanteau and scanned the room. "Hmmm, nice. Oh...you have two beds? Are you traveling with someone?" She was always too inquisitive—a fault to be sure—and she decided that she wouldn't blame the girl if she gave a rude reply.

A sweetness was all Lacey could detect in the girl's tone. "Yes, I am a traveling companion to Lady Stanhope. We usually take separate rooms but were told this was the last room available in the inn."

"I see. Well, I must be going," said Lacey as she moved toward the door. "Safe journeying..."

The girl's uneven steps followed. "Please...I don't even know your name...?" She was drawn to Lacey. She was a lonely girl and something in Lacey's personality had attracted her. She would have enjoyed sitting down to tea and a friendly chat . . . but of course that was impossible. She extended her hand. "I am Flora Morely."

Lace hated having to lie. "And I am Lace Eden." She smiled. "I really must go."

Flora returned the smile and though she would have liked to keep her there—gently as in all things she did—she allowed Lacey to go as quickly as she had appeared.

Chapter Four

A SERPENTINE OF silver weaved its way across neatly cut lawns slicing the road with little care. Sir Roland's eyes traveled its length as his coach rumbled over the small wooden bridge that joined the private road they would continue to travel. Lacey, opposite Sir Roland, had her face plastered to the window. She gazed on familiar scenes and remembered her youth. There, in the evergreen maze they had played at "horse n' hounds," there again ... the lily pond she and Buzzy had fallen into trying to walk along its edge on one foot! Ha, and he some eight years her senior! She could imagine her mother, with Father laughing in the background, rushing toward them ...

Those times were gone. She sighed. Ah, Bussingham Towers. It had been such a favorite haunt, for her mother and Lady Bussingham had been childhood friends and their friendship had lived through adulthood. Now, everything was changed. Her mother's death had done that...or rather, her father's remarriage. But no, she wouldn't dwell on it. She had to move forward with her age.

"There it is," said Sir Roland, bringing her out of her reverie. She had such a stricken, sad look in her eyes, and he had a sudden desire to bring her away from her thoughts.

She smiled, for he was referring to the mansion. It made quite an impressive show, set high among its rolling woodlands and parks. May flowers designed with skill in their well-ordered gardens were alive with colors as were the huge rhododendrons with their deep purple glory. Again she sighed, but this time she sat back and said to Sir Roland, "Whatever will Aunt Jana say when she sees me?"

"It is with some concern that I have been wondering just about the same thing, but what is more to the point...what shall we tell her?"

"Tell her? Why...the truth...but—" now she was thinking about her alias—"I had better see her alone first, don't you think?"

"That might be the wise course of action. Shall I stay in the stables until such time as you send for me?" He was being sarcastic but Lacey took him up at once.

"What an excellent notion to be sure. That is the very thing. You stay in the stables until I can explain everything..."

"I will do no such thing!" he snapped.

"But Sir Roland...think how awkward it will be...walking in together...?" The connotation was there.

He eyed her a long moment. "Very well. I shall give you five minutes..."

"Ten! Surely it will take five minutes alone just to explain about the highwaymen and all..."

"By Jupiter, girl, I think you have missed your calling! You should have gone into trade! Very well, then, ten minutes...no more!"

The Bussingham library had been outfitted much in the style of the day. A Regency table held the central focal point. Shelves of leather-bound volumes of various authors decorated the walls and two brightly printed silk sofas flanked the large, marble-framed fireplace. The lady of Bussingham Towers was at the moment pacing and attempting, at the same time, to dress down her only son.

"I am only thankful that your sister never gave me such cause for concern!" she snapped at a chance remark he had ill timed.

The viscount, ninth in his noble line, looked at his frenzied parent with amused affection. "But Mama, you are doing me up brown! Last I recall you were complaining that Sally sadly wanted spirit—"

"Never mind!" she snapped, cutting him off. She stood eyeing her son. She was a veritable Juno of a woman. Tall, elegant, lovely and quite capable at fifty of slaying as many hearts as she had when she was twenty. "We are discussing *your* faults *not* your sister's!"

His tongue found the hollow in his cheek and in mock meekness he said, "Of course, Mama...to be sure you are sadly worked, overset with a son such as I."

She wagged her finger at him. "You are a wonderful son, and well you know it. Now don't provoke me, Peter!"

"I wouldn't dream of it."

"Then answer my question, for I have not forgotten what it was I wanted to know, though you would have me take a wider road."

He sighed, "What, then?"

"The Winters woman. I asked you whether or not it was done?"

"Done?" He was finding her exasperation vastly amusing. He adored his mother but would on no account allow her to rule his affairs.

She found a spot above his fair curls and managed to control herself. She had gone to much trouble to get her son to accompany her to Bussingham Towers. She had had to feign illness, and just as the London season was going into full swing. Drat! But it was a sacrifice worth the making, if only to get him away from *that* woman! "Are you over her, Peter? Can you not give me an honest response?"

He said wearily, "Dearest, do you not realize that if I had been in love with Catherine Winters I would have asked her to marry me?"

She pulled a face. "My word Peter... you wouldn't... would you?"

He laughed at her expression. "I am afraid I would."

"But then... you do not love her? I rather thought..."

"I know what you thought. No, I realized what Catherine was very early in our relationship."

She pouted. After all, she had gone to a great deal of effort to snare him away from the woman! "Well, I must say, Peter, for someone whose heart was not in it, you did lead the lady on!"

He stared at her a moment in total astonishment and then gave over to a chortle of laughter with which he ended, "Catherine knew well the rules of our game, Mama, I promise you. She expected from me no less, no more than she received. Now, if you don't mind—"

He was interupted by the squeaking bark of a small animal and looked down to find a toy gray poodle doing circles 'round the room. "Buzzy... Aunt Jana... oh, pray, do forgive Peewee, he has been couped up for so long..." came the voice of a lively piece at the doorway. Lace went rushing forward because Lady Bussingham's arms were already extended. Lace had called her ladyship aunt from childhood and indeed felt closer to her than she did to any of her blood relatives.

"Lace... my sweet child... what has that dreadful woman done to you?" She was referring to the fact that Lace's appearance was intolerable, a fact she put at Lace's stepmother's door.

Lace immediately looked down at her breeches and smiled. "Well, she did not put me into these clothes... at least not directly, though in truth if she hadn't tried to force me to marry Collymore—"

"Hold!" This from the viscount, who moved forward and put his hand on Lace's curly head. Thusly he got her attention and disengaged her from his mother's arms. "You've put me all at sea girl! Now, slowly, tell me how you happen to be here."

She beamed up into his pleasant face. He was grave natured and more often than not quite capable of calling her escapades folly rather than fun, but he had been her friend as long as she could remember. She took up his hand and squeezed it and Lady Bussingham was struck not for the first time with an agreeable fancy. It would be so nice to have Lace as her daughter-in-law!

"Oh, Buzz... do not be angry. It could not be helped. I had to wear these clothes if I were going to

39

run away and make my way here."

The viscount found this explanation sadly lacking in information and exhibited his exasperation clearly. He was on no ceremony with Lace, for she had been too many times beneath his wing. "What is more to the point is how did you get here?"

"As it happens," offered Lace happily, "your friend brought me!"

It fell like a small bomb and had similar effects. *"What?"* said her audience in unison.

"Which friend?" demanded the viscount, his eyes narrowing.

"One of your closest friends, and I don't know what I would have done without him . . . for you must know that he chased off the highwaymen and—"

"Chased off the highwaymen?" squeaked Lady Bussingham, putting a hand to her fluff of silver-gold hair and doing its coiffure some minor damage.

"Hmm, yes . . ." said Lacey spying a sweetmeat and plopping it into her mouth. "They would have robbed me . . . and worse, but Sir Roland—"

Again she was cut off, this time by the viscount. *"Sir Roland?"*—and then with a hand to his forehead—"You say . . . Sir Roland. You have been in the company of Sir Roland . . . alone?"

"Why, yes, and he has been wonderful . . ."

"I have no doubt of that!" said Lady Bussingham on a rueful note. "He is reputed to be er . . . wonderful among the ladies. My dear child, you can have no notion being the innocent you are . . . but Sir Roland is quite a shocking rake!"

"Oh, yes, I know," said Lace, totally unconcerned by the fact. "He told me right off you know. That is why he kept me hidden half the time, sneaking me in and out of the inns . . . feeding me in the coach . . ."

"By Jupiter, I shall cut his throat!" snapped the viscount.

40

Round-eyed Lace appraised him. "Are you daft, Buzz? He helped me!"

"By...by...taking advantage of you?" returned his lordship on a blustering note.

Lace blushed hotly but she was angry too. She stamped her foot. "Stop it! I am past eighteen and you are not talking above my head. I may be green but not so much so that I don't know what I am about. He did not take advantage of me...sad to say he didn't even try!"

A twinkle lit Lady Bussingham's blue eyes and her arm went 'round Lace's shoulder. "How very mortifying for you to be sure," she said with quiet understanding.

Lace's dark eyes found her ladyship's. "Exactly. He thought me quite a youth...not a woman at all."

"Well, he was not given much of an opportunity to see you at your best, now was he?" returned Jana Bussingham.

"No, but I would have thought such a libertine as he is reputed to be, might have taken more notice of the fact that I am a female."

"What is this?" demanded the viscount in disbelief. "I find your attitude Mother...and yours Lace quite extraordinary!"

"Oh, don't be vexed, Peter," sighed Jana Bussingham. "It is above your understanding."

"Nevertheless, I intend to have Roland's head!"

"Do you? How disagreeable to be sure. I made certain this was the one place I would find sanctuary," said a strong male voice from the doorway.

"Confound it! Where the deuce is Buckles? Doesn't he announce anyone anymore?" complained Peter Bussingham in disgust.

"I sent the poor fellow off. After all...I know the way, Buzz old boy." Sir Roland gave his most charming smile. "And now, why is my head in danger of being taken off at Bussingham?"

Lady Bussingham wagged an admonishing finger at him. "Scamp! I don't know whether to scold you or thank you for bringing Lacey to us."

Lace interpolated quickly before he could respond, "'Tis your own fault! You promised ten minutes."

"I gave you ten minutes, minx," he answered, his eyes hinting his amusement. "You did not do very much with it."

"But I did, only Buzzy here insists that you have seduced me and all of my time has been wasted."

Sir Roland's eyes took on a hard glassy appearance as he scanned his friend's face. "Really...is that what you think, Buzz?"

The viscount frowned. No, he no longer thought any such thing; it was just that the entire episode was so improper and aggravating, he said only, "No, Roland, but—"

"Oh, don't bother me with buts. Do you or do you not wish to hear the whole?" said Lacey on an impatient note.

"Of course, dear," replied her ladyship. "Do tell us the whole."

Lacey turned to Sir Roland, "I need more than the ten minutes you gave me. Couldn't you... find your room...?"

He cocked his head. Why didn't she want him to hear what she had to say? Perhaps there were details too embarrassing for her to go into with a stranger present. Oddly enough, he felt a quick, sharp pang. She thought of him still as a stranger. He turned toward the viscount. "Is it the blue room for me?"

"Yes, as usual. You will probably find it all in readiness, for no doubt Buckles has had it attended to," answered the viscount gravely. "But Roland...it is not ended here!" There were still some things he would ask him.

"As you wish," said Sir Roland Keyes, his eyes gold flecked with his amusement.

Lace watched him go, admiring his broad shoulders as the door closed at his back. She sighed and then returned to her captive audience. "First, there is a promise I must extract from you."

"Of course, darling," said Lady Bussingham unhesitatingly.

"Not so fast!" returned her cautious son. "What sort of promise, Lace?"

"To keep my true identity a secret. I am here under an alias," she said on a hushed note.

"But why?" This from her ladyship.

"You see...Daphne was determined to marry me to Lord Collymore—"

"Fiend seize it! She can't..." interjected the viscount. He knew well that Daphne and Doug Collymore were lovers.

"So I told her. Daphne responded that she would ruin my reputation by saying that she had caught"— the heat rushed into Lace's cheeks—"that she had found me in a compromising situation with his lordship."

"Never say so!" exploded from both the viscount and his mother.

Lacey nodded her head. "It is so terribly mortifying, for it might be easily believed. I had something of a crush on Lord Collymore this past summer. A schoolgirl thing, you understand, and it was something I was totally over with by fall. Now, after all this time...so you see...I had to get away from her. I dressed in breeches from my groom, took Cricket and Peewee and...here we are. The rest you know."

Peewee heard his name and immediately lifted his head from its resting place near the fire. However, upon finding that no one paid him any mind, he sighed and dropped it down to the floor once again.

"But why the alias?" pursued the viscount, for his mother was still attempting to digest what she had been told and control her temper against Lace's stepmother.

"Oh. I told Sir Roland my name was Eden..."

"Your mother's maiden name?" This from Lady Bussingham.

"I thought it might be wiser to travel under an alias. I don't want Daphne to find me...not until I can discover a way of protecting myself from her schemes and besides..." she stopped herself, uncertain whether it was wise to go on.

"And besides what?" The viscount was watching her closely. One couldn't be sure what Lace was thinking. He knew her well and rarely did she do anything for the obvious reason.

"It is the best explanation I shall give you at the moment. Now will you keep my secret?"

"We shall have to warn Buckles of course..." said Lady Bussingham thoughtfully.

"My word! Mother, it is far more complicated than warning the servants to keep mum! Don't you see...? There will be outings and visitors...it poses all sorts of complications."

"Yes, but none that cannot be handled," answered his mother.

"I don't like it," pronounced the ninth Viscount of Bussingham.

"Oh, pooh!" returned his mother.

Chapter Five

LADY BUSSINGHAM STUDIED the silk pink roses she held up to the light beaming in from the shop window and called her youthful friend's attention. "Lace...these are perfect for the gown. Shall we take them or are they too extravagant?"

Lace looked up from the pile of gowns she had selected, many of which would have to be altered to her petite frame. "Hmmm, they are pretty, aren't they? Yes, why not add them to the collection." Her mind wandered to the problem of paying for all she had bought. She would have to apply to her barristers and that would mean letting them know her whereabouts. Could she count on them to keep silent? Well, she would have to work out this detail later. For the time being Lady Bussingham would lay the blunt. It was at about this moment of silent musing that she glanced lazily out the store window and discovered a familiar face looking in. Flaxen waves beneath a straw bonnet, soft blue eyes and a pert nose. It was Flora! Flora Morely whom she had met at the inn a few days back. Quickly she called to Lady Bussingham,

"I shall be back in a moment, Aunt Jana...do feel free to select whatever fripperies you feel I need..."

"But...don't you want to see...?" she called in some surprise as she watched Lace rush outdoors. Sighing over her young charge's vagaries she returned to the problem at hand. "I should like to see some ribbons as well," she asked of the saleswoman.

Flora had already stepped down the curb and was about to cross the busy cobbled street when a voice at her back halted her; she turned and found a young woman clothed in loosely fitting though fashionable shades of earthy colors chasing after her. It was not until Lace was upon her and taking up her hands that she recognized Lace as the young woman in boy's breeches who had extended her a kindness in the posting inn a few nights back.

"Why...Miss Eden..." She smiled with pleasant surprise lighting her face.

"Oh, don't be so stuffy," laughed Lace easily. "I called you Flora, did I not? Have you forgotten *my* given name?"

"How could I when you were so kind to me? I never dreamed we would ever meet again...or so soon?"

"Nor did I. How do you come to be in Nottingham?" asked Lacey curiously.

"Lady Stanhope has an estate just outside of town. I am of course staying with her." Flora's eyes had lost their sparkle.

Lace noted it, for she was ever sensitive to other's

46

moods; however, she meant to bring her new friend about. "Why, Flora, that is beyond everything famous. You must know that Bussingham Towers is but five miles off the main pike and that must make us neighbors. Are you free this afternoon? Can you return to Bussingham with us for high tea?"

Flora Morely sighed. "I am afraid I cannot, Lace. I am in town on an errand for Lady Stanhope and she expects me back shortly."

"Then tomorrow, Flora. You will come for tea tomorrow. I shan't take no for an answer. Bring her ladyship if you must...tell her an invitation has been extended to her through Lady Bussingham..." Seeing the doubt on Flora's face she patted her arm, "'Tis all right, I assure you. Now don't hedge, promise?"

"Oh...Lace...I...?" started Flora.

"Don't be difficult," argued Lacey amiably.

A smile flashed from the heart-shaped lips. "I shall try Lace and at any rate will let you know."

"Good, but don't just try Flora, *come!* I shall expect you."

Flora waved herself off on this note. She felt much more in spirits now than she had when she had started out for Nottingham alone in Lady Stanhope's curricle. The thought tickled her that although Lace Eden was now garbed in feminine attire, she still seemed rather strangely put together and she wondered if Lacey were some poor relation of Lady Bussingham.

Only obscurely aware that the spencer and gown she wore hung rather unfashionably 'round her figure, Lace bounced back toward the dress shop to gather up Lady Bussingham. She saw by the passing glances she received that Lady Bussingham's daughter's clothes were no longer the height of fashion and a giggle nearly escaped her. Ah, there were drawbacks to being an indigent relation; just see how people looked down their noses! But it was the role she had chosen to play!

In the parlor of the Burton town house Daphne Burton paced with some vexation. She turned her countenance and stared at a well-dressed though dandy-styled gentleman and observed through her momentary irritation that he was delightfully attractive. This fact caused her pulse rate to increase but she ignored it. Expressing her uppermost concern, she said, "Where can that brat be?"

The gentelman took a diminutive pinch of snuff from a gold snuffbox, breathed it rather long and languidly before snapping the lid of the box shut and brought his gaze to her face. "It doesn't really matter, my dear," he said.

"Not matter?" She was pouting. "I thought we agreed. You said yourself how convenient it would be to be married to my stepdaughter. It would allow us to be together so often without the least bit of talk."

"Would it? I doubt that, but as she has vanished, it seems rather out of the question now." The subject was beginning to wear. She had been harping on it for some days now. He was in fact becoming somewhat bored with Daphne in general. He needed a change and the thought flickered through his clever mind that a trip to the country might be just the thing.

She stamped her foot. She didn't like his attitude. "Douglas, you are being churlish! How dare you speak to me in that tone! It doesn't matter? I suppose *I* no longer matter to you?"

"You are allowing yourself to get worked up over nothing, Daphne. The girl has probably gone to one of her relatives. Give her time; she will return," he said as he began to rise.

"Where do you think you are going?" she snapped.

His eyes withdrew. "I was not aware that I was ever required to report my movements to you, my love."

She knew his character too well to press the point. She bit her lip. It was a sad thing to acknowledge that at last someone had such power over her but it was true—she was far more ensnared than he. Circumstances did not alleviate her problem, either. While her late husband had left her amply provided for, the bulk of the fortune had all gone to Lacey. What she received would be hardly enough to support Collymore's erratic and expensive habits! No, marriage with Collymore—even if he wanted it, which he did not—would be out of the question.

"I will see you again...soon...?" she cried on a hopeful note, for he was already at the door.

He smiled at her. No, he thought, no. By the time you send 'round a note begging me to call, I shall be well on my way out of London. He answered instead, "Of course, my love. Could I stay away from you?"

She was pleased with this and allowed him his exit without further argument, but as soon as he was gone she was assailed with certain doubts. He had not tried to touch her. Why? In fact, he did not seem as of late the bold, hot lover he had been. His eyes had ice to their grayness. There was a slight edge to his voice just before he left her. Drat! Could she be losing him? Devil take him, then...but please, please bring him back.

Sir Roland set his beaver top hat rakishly atop his auburn curls, smoothed back the silver tufts of hair at his temples and adjusted his greatcoat. However, just as he was approaching the large front door that Buckles moved to open for him a voice called him to a halt.

"Oh... are you going out?" It was Lace and her tone held disappointment of no little degree.

He looked up and nearly gasped. Was this the same schoolgirl who he had brought to Bussingham? Was this the same hoyden who had unconsciously bounced about through halls and rooms in clothes far too large to be anything but absurd? Gone was that minx and in her stead, a fashionable damsel all tricked out in fineries of the first stare! His astonishment showed all too clearly and she giggled at his expression.

"Ah, I see what it is, you are quite the snob! Did I look so very silly in Sally's clothes? I hadn't realized. I was only grateful that she had married and left them here, for if she hadn't I would have been forced to keep my breeches on all this while..." She was descending the stairs, coming toward him, twirling to give him various angles of herself. "A pretty gown, is it not?" she asked flashing a dimple, for she could see from his curving mouth that he thought it becoming.

His eyes traveled over her well-shaped neck, lingering but slightly on her full, youthful breasts swelling above the fashionably cut bodice, then down over her slimness which exuded sensuality in the tight lines of the well-fitting, pink-dotted muslin. Quickly he sent his eyes back to the face framed in chestnut curls which flopped about in short, wild and calculated disorder, giving her a hint of the bedroom and making her infinitely appealing to a man of Sir Roland's aggressive nature.

She was breathtaking, and she was quite out of his reach. Her innocence, her lack of fortune set her over the border. He had no intention of allowing his imagination to stray over Lacey Eden, he liked her too much to hurt her. However, he allowed himself a moment with her.

"You are quite ravishing, pet, and well you know it!" he told her as his eyes twinkled, and then he wondered how she had managed to pay for such a gown.

As though reading his mind she put in glibly, "Thank you, sir. It was very kind of her ladyship to lay the blunt for it, which is what she did for this gown and the others..."

"Others?" He was staring at her. "That was very generous of her indeed."

"Er...yes...'tis because of my mother, you know. Lady Bussingham and Mama had been friends all through childhood..." she added lamely and then to change the subject, "I see you are going out. Riding?"

"No." He flicked her nose with his finger. "You are a shade too inquisitive, my pet."

"You needn't tell me," she said quietly.

He had hurt her. Silly chit. "Don't be foolish; of course I needn't tell you," and then relenting, "I am going to pay a morning call...on my intended."

Lace's face fell. "Oh." It was all she could manage. "Well, then, don't let me keep you."

He hesitated, but then touching his hat he turned and was off. Lace heaved a sigh, noticed Buckles watching her from the door and sniffed. "Never mind," she told him, and stomped off before she could read the smile in his eyes.

Was he seeing correctly? Was this really Lacey coming toward him or a vision come alive from one of his fantasies? The Viscount Bussingham stood on the green lawns of his estate and watched in openmouthed stupefaction. In London he had seen her but a few times and then usually in Daphne's presence. She had always been clothed in schoolgirl gowns and it had been easy to think of her as the same young kitten he had known through youth. But now? Good God! Her breasts billowed above a flimsy gown of pink, her arms sweetly bare beneath the folds of a muslin shawl were white and tantalizing in their grace. Superb! Her hair? There was something different about the way its bouncing curls fell over her forehead, allowing her dark eyes to peep through. Seductive. Definitely seductive. Why...it was indecent!

She giggled at his expression. This was quite amusing, startling the men in her life. She rather liked it. "Buzzy...I came to walk with you. I hope you don't mind."

"Mind? No...but I say...did Mother say you could go about dressed like that?"

"She helped dress me, silly."

"Did she? By Jupiter." He thought on this. "Are you certain you haven't tricked her into allowing you to wear...*that?*" He made a motion over her gown.

"Trick her? Why should I? Buzz...I am well over eighteen, you know. How ridiculous to think I should still be going about in schoolgirl aprons! Now, walk with me and tell me what brought you and Lady Bussingham here, though I am grateful, for I don't know where I would have gone if you weren't here."

He relaxed. She did not look like his kitten but she still sounded like her. He took her hand through his arm and patted it. "There now, puss, what should bring us here but a need for some relaxation."

"Oh, that is a round tale if ever I heard one!"

declared Lace. "Now, truth, for I shan't be shammed."

"And that is no language for a young lady," he returned.

She sighed, "Shall I ever break you of the habit?"

"What habit?"

"Staidness," she returned at once.

This came as a shock to his lordship. He had always considered himself a jolly fellow, well able to fool with the best of them. He staid? Preposterous. His sister Sally was staid, but not he. "Really, Lace, that is coming on a bit too strong!" he declared in self-defense. "Staid indeed!"

"But Peter, you are...at least with me."

"Am I? I suppose you wouldn't think so if I were to let you have your head and run through the thicket?"

"Well, you are not my father...nor my brother..." she started.

"I am your friend!" he interpolated.

"Do you always instruct your friends how to go on?" she retorted, a brow raised.

He hedged. "Well...no...but..."

"Ah, then you should not be forever prosing to me. I am quite grown...perhaps a bit green but capable of handling myself all the same."

For the second time that morning Peter took a full look at Lacey and discovered a new and suddenly very attractive being. He retreated. This was dangerous. What was he doing? He was thinking of her as a woman, wanting her as a woman...this was madness. "Lace...I just thought of an errand I have to attend to. You will, I know, understand and excuse me."

"Of course." She was watching him rush off. How very odd. What had she done to upset him? Clearly this last exchange was contrived. It had been very pleasant to see the look of appreciation in his eyes. At last the Viscount Bussingham had recognized the fact that she was a woman, but instead of falling in with the remainder of her schemes he had scurried away. Why? And just what did she feel about him?

Chapter Six

LACE HAD WALKED for miles—or so it felt to her feet—in the new and somewhat crimping pink slippers she wore. Not the thing for a hike, she told herself ruefully. She had not intended to delve this deep into the woods but thoughts and time had gotten away with her. She sighed and took in her surroundings. The woods were bright with fat buds ready to open but the sun's position told her 'twas time to leave nature behind and return to Bussingham. Drat! What she needed was a shortcut through the fields. Her gown? She would have to protect its hem from the tall grass and low bushes. Well, nothing for it. She picked her way off the path toward the field fence, and balancing herself upon its weathered timbers, hobbled over to the other side. An open field lay ahead of her and she proceeded to climb up its slope, noticing for the first time a burst of color in the sky. Not any ordinary color but red, yellow and blue zigzagging in wayward stripes. What on earth...?

She stopped and stared, shading her eyes with her hand and tilting her head to get a better view. Something not quite round floated in the air space not far ahead. An uncommon thing but she knew what it was. She had never seen one before but she had heard about them. A balloon! "Bang up good luck!" she exclaimed out loud. "A real balloon!" Upon which she immediately forgot the state of her elegant dress and began scrambling to the peak of the slope.

"Hallo!" she cried at the back of a gentleman dressed only in shirtsleeves and pantaloons. "Why, this is beyond everything famous! Are you going to fly it?" She had all the ease of a child.

He turned. A man of average height with dark hair, dark eyes and a swarthy complexion. He was, upon first glance, not unattractive and when he smiled it lit up his face. "Hallo, and hopefully in time that is exactly what I shall do."

Lace immediately began to shower him with her limited knowledge of such things. "Hot air, isn't it? We talked about them in school but this is the first time I have ever seen one. Are you racing? Did something bring you down? How shall you get up again?"

He laughed easily, looking her over in his fashion. Pretty little thing, he thought. Such eyes...most devastating. "'Tis a hydrogen balloon, not hot air. Racing? No, though I should like to set a record, and yes, I was brought down because my partner fell ill which, as it turned out, was fortunate as I have discovered the balloon is in need of repairs."

"Oh...will you be able to manage by yourself...? I mean, with your partner on the mend and all?"

"It is proving to be difficult," he sighed.

"And where do you put this at night...to protect it?" She was as always too inquisitive to think of the proprieties.

He didn't seem to mind. "There is a shed not far from here." He gave her a thoughtful look. "I wonder if you might know where I could get some help? Perhaps a youth on your estate needing a few extra coins? You see, I am having trouble with this netting..."

She chuckled, "How do you know I have an estate?"

He looked her over purposely. "Don't you?"

She conceded easily, "As a matter of fact I am visiting on one. I am staying at Bussingham."

"And you are...?" Clearly he was boldly pushing forward but she had left herself open to this, he reasoned.

She hesitated. Whatever would Aunt Jana say to her standing in easy discourse with a stranger? Never mind, it was fun. "I am Lace Eden." What was the harm, she told herself, it wasn't even her proper name.

He bent gracefully over her hand. "Enchanted, Miss Eden." He was bringing his eyes to her face, allowing them to linger—a technique he had often found useful.

There was an intenseness in his gaze that frightened her into retreat. She took a step backward and withdrew her hand, telling herself she was behaving a silly miss. So she bucked herself up to ask, "...and you are?"

He smiled. "Mr. Charles Teggs."

"Oh, my goodness! I have heard of you! Didn't you fly your balloon the length of the channel?"

"I have the honor of claiming that," he said with a

57

modest inclination of his head. She was beginning to look like a possible conquest and he was beginning to enjoy the notion.

"Zounds!" was the lady's reply. "Just wait till I tell Buzzy! He is a balloon enthusiast, you know."

"Buzzy?" His eyes were quizzical, his lips curved. She was a delightful ingenue and he felt a sudden flaring of desire.

"The Viscount Bussingham. Oh, I can't tell you how thrilled I am to have met you. I must go now, for I am in a dreadful rush."

Again he inclined his dark head. "You will, I hope, try and send me someone...?"

"Yes, of course. Good-bye..." She was waving herself off.

He watched her go, his dark eyes bright before sighing and returning to his tangled webbing. Damn, but this was not going as quickly as he had anticipated. Well, there was nothing for it, he would simply just have to put in the time and hope the money would last. Lace's dark round eyes flashed in his mind. Enchanting wench and one he wouldn't mind bedding if he could. If he could? Damn, but when did he ever meet one he couldn't?

Lacey bounced into the hall and smiled at Buckles, who closed the front door behind her. "In the library?" she asked.

"Yes...Miss Eden, everyone is in the library having tea. Shall I announce you?"

"Don't be silly. I'll just go in," she said, rushing off.

The library door opened wide in her hand and she found three pairs of eyes, each holding a different expression. As usual Jana Bussingham was in a merry mood and quite pleased to see her favorite maid looking bright-eyed and rosy cheeked. Lord Bussingham's blue eyes were masked but there was something in his expression that puzzled her. He was excited about her appearance, she could sense it, yet there was something else in his air. Sir Roland's pleasure at her entrance was another thing altogether, for it tickled her into near delirium. Just why she should feel such palpitations simply because his eyes stroked her was beyond comprehension. No matter, it didn't signify. She had news to impart.

"Hallo. You will never guess what I have discovered!"

"Oh, my God!" groaned the viscount mockingly.

She pulled a face at him. "Just for that I shan't tell you and *you* would be sadly out."

"Never mind him," put in Sir Roland, going forward to take her hand and lead her to the sofa. "Come sit beside me and give me your news."

His touch. It sent a shiver through her. She set such sensations aside. "You, sir, are as always quite the gentleman. I don't know why it is that they say you are a rakehell, you don't seem so to me."

Lady Bussingham coughed deprecatingly. "Lace...er...do sit and tell us what it is you have discovered."

"All right," she said, plopping comfortably into the cushioned sofa, picking up an oriental silk throw pillow and setting it on her lap.

"I had been walking for an age. What with you busy with the household, Aunt Jana...Buzzy gone off somewhere...and Sir Roland gone"—she hesitated and then threw it out of her lungs—"gone courting, I was quite down..."

"You...down? Impossible," teased the viscount with a shake of his fair head.

"Well, I was, you horrid beast, so be quiet and let me finish." She waited for his total submission. "Now...where was I...?"

"Complaining about your lack of amusing companions..." put in Sir Roland goodnaturedly.

"I was *not* complaining! I, sir, do not complain. I was merely explaining how I came to be feeling out of sorts. Shh!" she added, for she sensed he was again about to interrupt. "Now...oh, yes. So then, off I went walking and before I knew what I was about...it was nearly tea time...and oh, is it still hot...?"

"Yes, dear, shall I pour you a cup?"

"Hmmm, please," she said before getting to the point, "and then there it was, you see."

"There what was?" asked the viscount.

"Thank you," said Lacey, taking the cup and then sipping at the hot, dark red brew. "The shortcut home brought me to it, you see."

"No, I don't think any of us sees," said Sir Roland, grinning impishly.

She didn't seem to mind his teasing. "The balloon! I thought at first it was a hot-air balloon but Mr. Teggs said he uses hydrogen..."

"Hold!" said the viscount. "What is this? Who is Mr. Teggs? What balloon?"

"Buzz, you can't mean to imply that *you* don't know who Charles Teggs is?" retorted Lace with some surprise.

"Charles Teggs? You saw Charles Teggs?" said the viscount dubiously.

"Excuse me my backwardness, but who is this fellow?" asked Sir Roland.

"He flew the coastline in his balloon," answered Lace excitedly. "And you will never believe it but he is quite young and personable. When I heard of it I was certain he was some sort of ruffian ... but it is no such thing."

"What does he look like?" asked her ladyship.

"Oh, he is rather dark ... and though not particularly handsome, very attractive, I think ..."

"Oh, do you?" returned the viscount on an odd note.

Sir Roland's eyes flew from the viscount's face to Lacey's and he took her attention on a quiet note. "I take it, then, that this Mr. Teggs has landed his balloon in the vicinity and that you came upon it this afternoon. How very exciting for you, minx."

She smiled gratefully at him. "I made certain *you* would understand."

"And I suppose I don't?" interjected the viscount. "Am I being staid and interfering because I think you shouldn't have stopped to converse with a stranger when you were alone simply because he landed in a balloon?"

Lace stared at him a long moment and then burst into indecent mirth, "Oh, Buzzy ... you do look ... so puffed up ..."

"Yes," agreed his mother. "Do come down." She turned to Lace. "Though ... he does have a point, dearest. It is not wise to allow yourself to be in a position whereby a ... a ... strange man may take ... er ..."

"Advantage of me?" put in Lace.

"Exactly so," said her ladyship.

Lace sighed. It was time to concede. No use fighting. She would not win and it didn't matter. In the end she would do what her own mind dictated. "I suppose you have a point."

"Damn, but I am glad that is settled," said Buzzy and then added, "Hydrogen, you say?"

"Yes, and his basket was shaped like a boat. He

61

stores it overnight in a shed not far from where I met him. I imagine he is staying at a local inn."

"Oh!" interjected her ladyship, putting her hand to her cheek. "I nearly forgot. A messenger came from the Stanhope Estate...and I must say, Lace, I was most surprised, for I have no use for Lady Stanhope and cannot imagine why you extended an invitation in my name to that woman...but at any rate, she sent a reply saying she could not make tea today but would try tomorrow. It is most vexing as I don't want her today or tomorrow."

Lace laughed. "Oh, poor Aunt Jana...I am sorry, but it was the only way I could think of getting Flora here."

"Flora?" chimed both her ladyship and the viscount. Sir Roland, sitting back and watching, found his minx at work was a comedy he wouldn't miss for the world. Then he thought of Miss Letty Rainbird, the new object of his attention, and he felt a quiet shudder before he dismissed her from his mind.

"Oh, I had forgotten to tell you about Flora Morely. She is Lady Stanhope's companion and I mean to make a friend of her. I know you will like her immensely and, oh, Aunt Jana...she is so terribly lonely. I just had to rescue her."

"Of course you did, my dear."

"Mother!" Peter Bussingham was genuinely shocked. "We cannot encourage Lace into a friendship with a hired companion!"

Lady Bussingham found herself in some confusion. On the one hand her son was right. Propriety forbade the fraternizing of aristocracy and those less fortunate. On the other hand, Lace needed a friend her own age, and she did feel rather sorry for any young woman having to work for Lady Stanhope. "No...but, Peter, don't you think...?"

"No, I do not!" snapped her son. "Please let me hear no more about such nonsense."

"Don't pay Buzzy any mind," said Lacey not in the least perturbed. "He shall come 'round, you know."

He did come 'round, on her, his eyes glaring. He wanted to shake her. He looked at her hard and found instead, quite suddenly, that he wanted to kiss her, touch her...damn...what was happening? He restrained his emotions and his words came carefully.

"Lace...don't you see? All I want to do is protect you."

She smiled warmly at him. "Indeed I see very well. Dear Buzz, Flora Morely is a very decent sort, you cannot..."

"That is not the point!" interjected the viscount. "You must stop attaching yourself to every stray that comes along."

"What a horrid thing to say," returned Lace finally getting angry. "If more people took in strays there would not be any!"

"I think..." said Sir Roland, and again his quiet authority took command of the room, "that all of you are making too much out of this. I am certain Lady Stanhope's companion will meet with your high standards and at the same time afford our Lace a good friend."

"Oh, is that so, Ro? Just how do you know that?" asked the viscount on an irritated note.

"Because I am acquainted with the lady," he said gravely.

A silence most deafening in its intensity met this remark. Lace was the first to break it. "You know Flora?"

He nodded but before he was allowed to elaborate on this the viscount broke in with a snort, "And I suppose that puts the lady above suspicion?"

"Sarcasm does not look well on you, Peter," said Sir Roland dryly. "You should try and cultivate your sneer, it is far too pronounced."

"But how do you know her?" asked Lace attempting to return to the point at hand.

"I was acquainted with her brother, Lord Davenport," he said, giving her a warm smile.

"Davenport?" ejaculated the viscount.

"My word," said his mother, "but...he was killed in a duel last year..."

"How dreadful," said Lace.

"Exactly so, for his house was not in order at the time. His estates were to let and his sister was left penniless. I believe that friends set Miss Morely up with references and she went to Lady Stanhope."

"But you never said a word...I mean, you must have seen her at the inn...on our way...the night I met her..." put in Lace.

He smiled benignly. "I saw her and thought it best that she did not see me...under the circumstances."

"I see," said Lace quietly. For no reason at all she suddenly felt depressed. "I am feeling somewhat tired. I think I'll go to my room," she said, starting to get up.

Sir Roland was on his feet immediately and bending over her hand. What was wrong? Why had her eyes taken on such a look? What had he said to disturb her? He compensated for his doubts by touching her nose. "Till later, pet."

She brightened at once and the next moment she was bouncing out of the room. He watched her go. Odd. She was in a way peculiar to herself, totally captivating, and if he wasn't careful he would find himself in terrible straits. He could ill afford that now. A sigh escaped him.

"All right, then," said Lady Bussingham returning to the subject they had begun before Lace's entrance, "how did you like Miss Letty Rainbird?" There was a tease in her voice which expressed her own views of the young woman.

He pulled a face. "A curious question when you know that I am going to marry the wench."

"By Jupiter!" ejaculated the viscount. "You haven't popped the question to her already?"

"Don't be a dunce," returned Sir Roland.

"Then you don't know she will accept," retorted the viscount. "Might have other notions in mind." Though he doubted this. Letty Rainbird was not to his taste and he could not therefore imagine she had any list of suitors.

"When I ask her...she will accept. And by the by, Buzzy, she is far more attractive than you painted her."

"Oh, stop!" demanded her ladyship. "Letty Rainbird attractive? Don't be absurd. She may have some countenance but there is that in her character that puts one off."

"Yes, that's true, Ro...damn, but I never thought you would go through with it once you'd met her," said the viscount, shaking his fair head. "She is just not in your usual style."

"What is in my style is her pockets," said Sir Roland dryly.

Lady Bussingham leaned over and rapped his knuckles with her tight fan, "Horrid scamp!"

"Much worse than that, madam..." sighed Sir Roland, thinking on what he was, still more disturbing, what he was becoming. He leaned back against the sofa and found the leaping flames of the fire in the grate. Life was beginning to wear hard, and then he heard Lacey's voice outside the library doors.

"Peewee! Confound you! Peewee...don't you dare

do that on the nice polished floors!" She saw that he had not heeded her and sighed, "Drat!"

And Sir Roland found himself smiling in spite of his despondent mood!

Chapter Seven

LETTY RAINBIRD'S PALE gray eyes narrowed into slits of ice. It was always so when her mind was hard at work, as it was now. She was watching Sir Roland as he adjusted his shirt cuff beneath the buckskin folds of his riding coat. He was certainly a well-formed man, tall, arrogantly self-assured. She would have preferred him to be a lord, a marquess...but even so, his title was not to be despised. Sir Roland Keyes. It was amusing to think of herself as his lady.

He looked her way as he crossed the pebbled courtyard to assist her to mount her horse and she gave him a dazzling smile, patting her auburn curls beneath her dark riding hat all the while.

"Lud, but I do think you have chosen a perfect day for riding," she said sweetly. "I only hope you won't be bored with country roads, sir," she said, deliberately baiting him.

He was not backward in responding. "Now, Miss Rainbird, tell me how I may be bored when in your company?"

She tittered admirably and put a gloved hand to her mouth. He found himself disliking the affectation, but never mind, she was certainly well formed and there was that about her that hinted of warm blood. He wondered for a moment what it would be like to hold her tall, graceful body in his arms? He was bending to give her a leg up and she was pursing her lips flirtatiously.

"How strong you are, sir," she said, her voice low.

"How light you are, love," he answered, his voice on par with her own.

She smiled to herself. He was already becoming familiar. Good, she rather liked dallying with this one. As she busied herself with her thoughts and her plans, she did not realize that her heels were digging into her mare's girth. The mare reacted; she responded by yanking hard on the reins and the mare's head went up as the bit tortured her mouth. "Bad Dusty!" snapped Letty. She was spoiled in all ways and unable to support opposition of any kind. Her hand slapped the mare's neck with the sharp-toned reprimand.

Sir Roland was horrified. She was no horsewoman and the fine steed she rode would be ruined by such hands. He attempted to curb her active arms. "There, Miss Rainbird ... if you will but point in your toes she will not want to go with you." He was touching her elbow, urging her hands down as he spoke.

Letty did not like being told but she restrained the sharp retort that came to mind. With a slight edge, she replied, "Really, Sir Roland, I have been riding since I was ten years old!"

"I am sure you have," said Roland, his eyes saying much more than his words as he went to mount his own bay gelding. For the tenth time that morning he reminded himself that his estates were to let, that her money was no longer just a desirable asset, but a necessity!

He brought his bay abreast and smiled at her. "Well, now, my fair charmer, you have a free hand for I am unfamiliar with your countryside, and intend to ferret out both its secrets and yours!"

She giggled. "Why, sir...what secrets could we have up here?"

"For one, how have you managed to remain unattached?" He was curious on this point, for with her fortune and her attractiveness it was something of a surprise to know that she had not ensnared a husband during the London season.

She hesitated. It was most humiliating to reflect on last season. What must she do but fall in love with a penniless, shiftless being who proved himself false? But she had learned. Her papa had taught her well. Never mind, that was over and a year had passed, a year in which she had found her green heart green no more and her ideals altered. "I did not find myself attached to any of the young men I met during my season."

"And you would have to find yourself...attached, before committing yourself to marriage?"

Was he mocking her? Didn't he believe her? What was it she read but did not understand in his tone? She answered slowly, "To some extent certainly, however my father would have to approve of the match and *he* has very high ideals for me."

"How fortunate for me that he has not removed you to London once again," said Sir Roland, but again his tone was unfathomable.

She looked at him sideways meaning to flirt but not quite sure of him yet. "Mama is not in good health...I do not expect another London season until next year."

"Don't count on it, my dear, you will be snapped up long before then," said Sir Roland, allowing his eyes to hint at his meaning.

Letty Rainbird smiled to herself. He was a charmer this one. She was not fooling herself. He was here because of her money...but he was quite willing to fall under her spell. She must only learn the knack of conjuring one up!

The warm breeze was invigorating, glorious, thought Lacey as the sun's spring rays engulfed her in light. She was looking quite the picture in her blue silk top hat with its pale scarf floating along her back and her chestnut curls peeping beneath its rim. A matching riding habit cascaded along her horse's withers and down his flanks and her gloved hands moved, giving and taking with the pull of his neck. She rode Cricket in a smooth, collected canter across the fields and they were as one being rolling and lifting with the flow of the land. His black ears were up to the sound of her crooning and his long, black tail swished in the breeze.

Riding like this always brought an unconscious smile to her lips but in contrast were her dark-winged brows, for they were drawn in a frown. Lacey was troubled by a flood of thoughts. How do you know what you feel this time is any different from what you felt for Doug Collymore? They are not unalike? I know, she answered herself, I just know. What is the good? He is a fortune hunter...courting another woman. Tell him the truth...he will court you? Never! Not that way...she didn't want him that way. And what of Buzz? What are you feeling for Buzz? I don't know, I don't know! Better to forget both men and concentrate on Charles Teggs!

That was precisely her decision as she made her way toward him. She could see him bending over his work. He was well formed. She could see the firm muscles in his back and arms. He was unbending, looking her way. His arm was going up...waving. He was smiling and well pleased to see her. Good! Charles Teggs was just the diversion she needed!

"Miss Eden...what an unexpected pleasure!" he called to her.

She was out of breath from the exertion of the canter across the field, her cheeks were in bloom, her eyes bright and the total picture breathtaking. She saw the look of appreciation in his eyes and felt a surge of gratification.

"Hallo! I thought I'd ride by and tell you to expect one of the Bussingham grooms. I spoke with him...His name is Jonas, by the way, and he said he would be happy to do what he could to help you."

"However can I thank you?" he said coming toward her. She was riding on a lady's saddle and he reached up for her waist.

She eyed him a moment. She was used to dismounting herself and she sensed a certain forwardness in his move. There was more than chivalry involved here, but...why not? She allowed him to take her waist in his strong grasp and lift her slowly to the ground.

"As light as..." he started.

"Don't you dare!" She laughed.

He joined her. "Quite, but nevertheless a pleasurable handful."

She moved her head sideways and walked a pace away from him. "Oh, my," she said pointing to her find, "these ropes are not only tangled but frayed as well!"

He sighed, "Indeed they are and the devil to mend. You see, this netting goes 'round the entire balloon and keeps the basket in place. I'm afraid they are going to take me somewhat longer to repair than I had at first anticipated."

The sound of a horse's hooves stalled her response and brought her head 'round. She saw a lone male rider coming toward them and he looked in a black mood. As he approached she put up a welcoming hand.

Viscount Bussingham slowed his pace. It would not do to come upon them at a full gallop. It was irritating though to see her standing so close to the fellow. She appeared to be already on intimate terms. Most aggravating...but why? He slowed his horse to a standstill, and there was about his mouth a sharp line of disapproval. However, his tone to Lace when he spoke was gentle enough.

"Lace, dear, I didn't know you wished to ride out this morning. Why did you not send word to me? I would have gladly dropped everything to accompany you." There was a hint in his tone of hurt and an implied reprimand as well.

She eyed him a moment. Her Buzz was acting very strangely as of late. "But Buzz...you were closeted with your man of business. I could not disturb you ...especially when it wasn't necessary. Now that you are here, however, do get down and meet Mr. Teggs..."

There was nothing for it. He had little choice. He could order Lacey to mount and accompany him away from this casually dressed chap, however, he was quite certain she would embarrass them all by refusing such a command; or he could comply with her wishes. He slipped nimbly off his steed and came forward as Lace happily made the introductions.

"Lace tells us that you are down for repairs...?" said Buzz with some interest as he gazed at the balloon.

Mr. Teggs admitted that this was true and began to move away, politely indicating that he wished to return to his work. The truth was he was rather displeased with the viscount's arrival on the scene. Lace was a subject worthy of pursuit. However, he could see the viscount would present difficulties. This conclusion made the entire scene he now found himself in rather more than boring.

With Mr. Tegg's retreat came the viscount's onslaught. "Fascinating, your occupation, I mean," said Buzz on a wistful note. "I have always thought you balloon fellows devilishly lucky flying up there among the clouds."

"Yes... but how do you control things... from the clouds?" asked Lace joining them.

Mr. Teggs smiled at her. Such full sweet lips, he thought as he answered, "In simple terms it is a matter of making the balloon lighter to rise... heavier to descend."

"Oh... thus the sandbags," concluded Lace. "But after you have dropped all the sand... you have no weight to get you back down. I don't understand."

He laughed lightly and had an urge to trace her pursed lips with his finger. He restrained himself and answered her instead. "There is a valve, Miss Eden, which, when opened, releases some of the gas. The less hydrogen the balloon has the more it will drop."

"But ... how do you control your direction ...?" she pursued.

"That is a bit more complicated. We have so many factors to contend with, you see. However, it works on the same principle as lowering or raising the balloon. At different heights the wind blows in different directions. It is sometimes a thing of trial and error to put the balloon at the correct height for the route you wish to forge."

"It seems all very precarious to me," said Lace doubtfully.

"Yes, but gloriously exciting," responded Mr. Teggs.

Again came the sound of horses' hooves cutting turf and they looked 'round to see two more riders approaching. Lace knew one of them instantly and her face lit up, then she saw his companion. Sir Roland and Miss Rainbird were coming upon them. She moved back as the viscount went forward to greet them.

Mr. Teggs seemed fascinated with the new arrivals. He could not tear his gaze away and Lace had to repeat her words twice to get his attention. "I said you are being bombarded today ... Mr. Teggs?"

"What ... oh ... yes," he said absently and then added, "Friends of yours, Miss Eden?"

"As a matter of fact ... the gentleman is ... but I am not acquainted with the lady." She was watching him closely for certainly he was behaving strangely nervous.

"Lace ...?" called Sir Roland, leaving his feminine companion in the viscount's care to come forward and take her hands. "What is it? Has Buzz foiled your attempt to take off in a balloon?"

"Don't be nonsensical!" She rapped his hand and turned to introduce him to the balloonist at her side. Then, as an afterthought, "It would be exciting...?"

Mr. Teggs laughed and shook his head. "Rule number one, which I shall never break, is that no females come on board!"

"Why of all the dreadful things to say!" exclaimed Lacey.

The viscount had Miss Rainbird's elbow and was leading her toward Lace. "And I want to make known to you a long-standing family friend, Miss Lace Eden..." He felt a wave of shame as Lace's alias rolled off his tongue but there was nothing for it. "...Miss Letty Rainbird."

Lace smiled amicably enough but as she looked at the young woman before her she felt an instinctive dislike. Stop it! You mustn't feel that way. It is most unfair. You have only just met her; you must give her a chance. And still she could not like her.

Miss Rainbird was paying Lace little mind. Her eyes were on Charles Teggs's face. She was being introduced to him and a close observer would have noted that her cheeks went white.

"I rather fancy... Miss Rainbird and I have already met," said Mr. Teggs, his tone unreadable.

"How... good of you to remember," responded Letty Rainbird, her mouth curving on a sardonic note.

Sir Roland's interest was caught and he looked from Charles Teggs to Letty with curiosity. These two knew each other...? This fact was not lost on Lacey either and she caught Sir Roland's eye.

"You are jesting, of course, Miss Rainbird. Could any man forget the pleasure of having met you?" said Mr. Teggs.

She tittered and moved away from him, but her bitter whisper met his ears as she passed his shoulder. *"Liar!"*

"I have a notion, Buzz!" ejaculated Lace. "Let us all ride into Nottingham and have lunch at one of those little tearooms."

"Hmmm...I don't know..." hesitated Buzz.

"I think Lace has hit upon an excellent notion," agreed Sir Roland. "Does it meet with your approval, Miss Letty?"

"Sounds utterly delightful," responded Letty on a sarcastic note.

"If you would rather I return you to your home?" said Sir Roland, his tone cold.

Her mouth moved petulantly. "Oh, if everyone is for it, then so must I be."

"How good of you," said Sir Roland dryly. He turned to Mr. Teggs. "Do you join us, sir?"

Charles Teggs smiled regretfully. "No, I'm afraid not, but enjoy, enjoy."

"We will," said Letty Rainbird the false sweetness dripping thickly.

Lace eyed her strangely. What was it between Miss Letty and Mr. Teggs? Again she found Sir Roland's eyes but Mr. Teggs caught her by the elbow and drew her away from her friends. "Miss Eden...you will stop by and keep me company again, won't you?"

She dimpled, "If you like."

"I do," he said emphatically.

"Then I shall."

Sir Roland heard this exchange and once again leaving Letty to the viscount he moved toward Lace. "Come, let me help you with your horse."

"I must tighten the girth...I loosened it earlier..."

"Never mind. I'll do it," he said, lifting her in his strong arms and perching her in her sidesaddle.

She watched him as he worked the girth buckles and before she could stop herself said, "Sir Roland...I don't like her."

"Don't you? How fortunate, then, that you shall not have to marry her," he answered sharply and then walked away.

She watched him for a long moment feeling something of hurt shoot through her. Did he already care for Letty Rainbird? Did he care so much that he would hear nought against her? A most unhappy thought indeed.

Sir Roland mounted his bay. He had been rude to Lace. Why? Because he was caught in a bind and because she had pinched that bind. He looked back and saw her face, her eyes. What was it about her that drew him? No answer. He only knew he couldn't leave her like that to take up position next to Letty. He allowed the viscount to take his place and urged his horse to reach Lace.

He smiled at her. "This is the first I have seen you in a sidesaddle. You sit it well."

"Thank you. It is Lady Bussingham's. I prefer riding astride but she would not hear of it. Said I must wear this habit and ride like a lady." She sighed.

"It is all very depressing, isn't it?" he teased.

She looked at him sharply. "What is lowering is the fact that time goes on but nothing changes for a woman. We must do this and that simply because that's the way it has always been, not because it is right!"

He laughed. "What? Have I opened a Pandora's box. I had no idea you were simmering with such juices."

She grinned at him. "And I rather thought *you* knew what I was about."

He looked at her for a long moment and then before

77

he could stop himself, "You said...on our way to Nottingham that you might consider marrying Buzzy. Are you still of that mind?"

She frowned. "Why do you feel free to inquire into my affairs and yet bar me from yours?"

"Whatever do you mean?" he returned, eyeing her doubtfully.

"Oh, don't act so surprised, Sir Roland." She sighed over the problem, wondering how to put this. "A few moments ago I ventured an unfavorable opinion on Miss Rainbird. Perhaps I was out of line. I don't think so. It is not as though you are in love with the wench, now is it?" She looked sideways at him. "Or is it?"

"I never tried to pretend that my suit for Miss Rainbird was prompted out of...er...esteem. How could I when I have only just met the woman?"

"Then why did you shut me out? Why didn't you inquire what prompted my opinion?"

He let go an exasperated sigh. "Because I don't wish to discuss the matter with you, minx!"

"Ah. That is of course your right. It is also my right to withhold my own news."

"So then you are refusing to tell me whether or not you mean to make a push at Buzzy?"

She put up her chin. "If I were a man I would knock you down for that! Make a push at him indeed!"

"I do beg your pardon. I seem only capable this morning of offending you. Perhaps it would be better if I sent the viscount to keep you company."

"I think it would be much better," she said on a quiet note. So he was put out with her. Very well, if that was what was needed, so be it. She watched him trot his horse up ahead and take Buzzy's place beside Miss Rainbird. Drat the man!

Chapter Eight

LORD COLLYMORE LEFT Lady Stanhope's plush stables at his back and with a heavy sigh took his steps toward the large Gothic house. It was insupportable that she should be so wickedly wealthy and he should be reduced to beggarly pursuits. Lacey Burton had dashed his hopes. He had never dreamed the chit would refuse his suit. But looking back on the last nine months told him a story. She had grown colder with the coming of winter and she had not thawed in the spring. Was it possible that she had found out about his relationship with her stepmother? Again the sigh. Damn Daphne her looseness. If she had been more careful he would now be on his honeymoon making love to as enchanting a little bird as ever he had come across and he would have had the comfort of knowing that his pockets were well lined! Ah, well, it was his ill luck that his charm and cunning had not brought him 'round. Once again he would have to apply to Lady Stanhope for a loan.

Damn the old witch! She was his aunt by marriage, for she had been married to his mother's brother. He was a favorite with her and he knew well the reason for this. He was the very likeness of his late father and Lady Stanhope had always been overly fond of that gentleman!

The front door of the stately mansion opened to his knock and Lord Collymore found himself putting his hat and greatcoat into the hands of a porter. The man was a stranger to him, a new addition to his aunt's household no doubt, yet, there was something familiar about him.

"Good-day to you," said his lordship. "I am Lord Collymore, her ladyship's nephew." Before the porter could comment on this, he continued, "Tell me ... are you new here ... or is it my lamentable memory that fails me?" He was quite sure his memory was not at fault but he wanted to hear the man speak to better place him, for he was now quite certain he had seen him somewhere other than his aunt's establishment.

The porter was a large, gruff man with a shock of unruly steel-colored hair now open to inspection as he kept his head bent and his gaze averted. "That's the way of it, m'lord. New I am," said the man as cheerfully as he could under such close scrutiny.

"Well, then, since I have given you my name, perhaps you will find it pleasant to do the same," said his lordship sardonically cold.

"Stills, it be, m'lord. Be there anything else ye'd be wanting of me?" Clearly he wished to escape.

"Yes, my aunt's whereabouts if you please?"

"She be in the Yellow Saloon, m'lord." He looked up and found with some undisguised relief the butler coming toward them to take over the situation. He backed off and slinked into obscurity.

Frowning, Lord Collymore dismissed the problem of placing Stills and gave himself over to the butler's show of welcome. So much nicer to have familiars about to pay him the proper respect, he thought as he followed the man to the Yellow Saloon.

In properly reverent tones the butler announced his lordship. Flora looked up from the book she had been reading aloud to her ladyship and saw an extremely well-dressed and rather polished young man coming toward them. His coat of blue superfine fit to perfection his slim, well-shaped torso as did his tight-fitting biscuit breeches. His Hessians sparkled as did the few well-appointed fobs at his waist. She managed to bring her eyes to his face and there found pleasant features framed in a Brutus-style hairdo the color of sunlight brown. She found the results of her appraisal brought a flush to her cheeks and she knew not where to look as he rewarded her with a similar survey.

"Collymore!" called Lady Stanhope joyfully. "So, you decided to follow me to Winter Oaks after all?"

He came forward and took up her hands putting them to his lips and softly offering her a kiss. "Dearest Carmen," he murmured, for he had long been aware that she was in her own way quite taken with him. It would never do to call her aunt! "How could I stay away? Once you had left London there was nought I could do but follow you."

Her cheeks were heavily rouged and as she pursed her lips it had a repulsive effect. "Liar!" she bantered, feeling quite a girl again. "Ah, but such a good one. Come, sit down beside me and give me your news."

He glanced toward Flora. Quite a little beauty his aunt had found herself, but clubfooted, he had heard.

81

This was the first he was seeing of her. "Are you certain I am not interrupting . . . ?" Clearly he wanted an introduction.

Carmen Stanhope's faded hazel eyes narrowed. She scanned his countenance carefully and her hand played idly with the dangling gold chain about her neck. She liked Flora Morely and she didn't want to have to let her go. She was a good girl, and while Carmen Stanhope was basically a selfish woman she rather liked the role she now played as Flora's benefactor. She had taken Flora in as a companion only one month ago and the girl had actually taken her fancy. But now here was her favorite rake looking far too interested in the chit. She wouldn't have it. "You are not interrupting. Flora, this is my nephew Lord Douglas Collymore. Doug, dear, this is Flora Morely, she has come with me as my companion." She turned again to Flora and her eyes held cold dismissal. "Well, child, you shan't have to accompany me to Bussingham now that Collymore is here; you may go."

"Oh . . . but . . ." started Flora.

Her ladyship's brow went up but there was no inquiry in her eye. She was displeased and considered Flora's mild objection a show of insubordination. "I said you may go, dear." Her tone was cold.

Flora nearly jumped to her feet. She was heated from the top of her head to the tips of her toes. Would she ever get used to the mortification of it all? Reduced from petted child of nobility to this? She made a hasty curtsy and hobbled from the room, all too aware of Collymore's eyes at her back. How she hated her foot! How ashamed she was of the style of her walk.

Lord Collymore waited for the door to close behind

her. "Such a shame about her foot, for the chit has real beauty otherwise."

"Never mind, Colly..." said Lady Stanhope, patting the cushion nearest her.

The sunshine felt warm and inviting as Lace preceded the viscount out of the Bussingham stables. She took in a long whiff of air and wondered what Sir Roland was saying to Miss Rainbird now. He had left them at the crossroads to escort Letty home, and she had been trying to dismiss him from her thoughts ever since.

Buzz came up behind her and she gave him a long, warm grin,

"It was a nice day...in spite of Miss Rainbird, wasn't it?"

He beamed. "By Jove, Lace, when the waiter spilled the glass of lemonade down her gown I thought for certain you were going to let go and laugh."

"Oh, I nearly did. If I hadn't caught your grave expression I am certain I would have forgotten myself, for you know I can't like the girl."

He sighed, "I am afraid I'm with you there. But..." He took up her hand. "Come on...let's forget Miss Rainbird, the lemonade and Sir Roland for a time."

"Oh, this sounds serious. I hope you are not going to read me another lecture?" she teased.

He stopped and pulled her 'round to look at him. "Am I really all that bad, Lace?"

She reached up and touched his face. "Oh, no...of course not, Buzz."

They were partially concealed by the row of rhododendrons that lined the walk. It was the moment. He knew it was the moment if only he could keep himself from botching it. "Lace...I have been waiting for you to be still long enough for me to tell you..." He stopped, unable to go on.

"Well...to tell me what?"

This was the moment, he repeated to himself. He slipped his arm 'round her waist and drew her near. "To tell you, Lace, that you have grown far too beautiful to resist..."

His kiss was not frightening, but neither was it passionate. He was a man suddenly overwhelmed to find that a being he had always cherished as a youthful friend had quite turned things about. Suddenly she was a sensual creature emitting bewitching sounds, moving in infinite grace. Lacey was losing the aura of childhood friend and becoming instead an intensely desirable woman. Now this posed a problem and hence his black moods of late. One can not after all make passionate love to a friend, yet this friend was different and he needed to express something of what he felt. Hence the kiss, tame in its nature, perhaps meant as an opening for more and then stilled in its birth.

Lace drew back cautiously and looked up at his face. "Oh, dear, what shall I do?"

This was not what he expected, nor what he wanted. "What do you mean?" he demanded.

"Now, Buzz, don't get yourself into a pucker. You kiss very nicely but you don't really mean it, do you?"

What the devil did she mean he kisses very nicely? He was wont to think of himself as exceptional! He took umbrage. "Mean it? By Jupiter, girl, why would I have kissed you if I didn't mean it?"

She sighed, "Oh, I expect I look rather different all trussed up and fashionable. You were wont to see me dressed in the gowns that Daphne chose for me." She patted his arm. "But never mind, I expect you'll grow used to it."

He was furious. He didn't go about kissing every attractive female he saw. He took such things far more seriously than that and so he would show her! "Damn it, Lace! Can't you see how I feel about you?"

"Yes, a sight better than *you* do, I am afraid," she answered.

Well, then, he would just have to show her! Again his hand found her small waist but this time his grip was firmer, his hold aggressive as he bent her beneath his body. His mouth took its objective, parting her lips with decisive determination and rather more defiance than lust. He was well satisfied with his form of instruction when he came away.

Breathlessly Lacey finally found herself free but before she could comment a hard, caustic male voice sent a shiver through her entire being.

"I see I am interrupting," sneered Sir Roland. "Shall I go away?"

Lace found his face and there discovered his lips drawn in a hard, frigid line. His eyes were glittering with jaggard specks of gold. He was blistering but with what? Disapproval. "Sir Roland..." she breathed, for nothing else came through, only his name. She felt as though her cheeks were on fire.

"Go away, Ro!" snapped Buzzy, for he was himself far too worked up to note his friend's hard mood.

"Indeed? Shall I go away, Lace?" There was an intenseness in his question that left her knees weak. How dare he? How dare he disapprove! He was off courting some horrible girl for financial advancement and here he was convicting her without the facts. It was the outside of enough! However, rescue came. A sharp bark brought her head 'round to find her miniature poodle wagging his puffed tail.

"Peewee!" she exclaimed thankfully. "Come on ...let's go." She ruffled his head as she lifted him to her face. "Poor boy. Have I been neglecting you?" With which she gave her back to the two furious gentlemen, neatly sidestepping the scene.

Sir Roland and the Viscount Bussingham eyed one another askance but neither chose to speak. In silence they followed in Lace's wake.

Some hours later the sun was setting. High tea was upon them and the clock about to strike the hour of five. Lacey observed these facts as she gave her bright chestnut curls one final pat and smoothed her hand over her pale green velvet gown. She was well pleased with the reflection she cast in the long looking glass, and with a light skip she left the room.

Downstairs she found the parlor empty and with a shrug looked in at the library. The doorknob was still in her hand as she looked across the room and found Sir Roland. Why did she feel this way? Why did her heart bounce inside? Why did she feel the blood rush to her cheeks? This was Sir Roland. He was her friend. He had helped her to arrive at Bussingham safely. He was going to marry Letty Rainbird.

"Aren't you going to come in . . . or are you still in a miff with me?" he asked gently. Something had wedged itself between them and it was threatening to destroy the cord of easy friendship they had enjoyed. What was it?

She smiled warmly and entered the room leaving the door partially ajar. She saw that his eyes noticed this and felt ashamed. Why did she feel at a loss for words? This was not like her.

"I am famished," she said at last.

He burst out with a hearty chuckle. "Aren't you always, minx?"

"Yes, I am. Do you think I have a worm inside taking everything I send for and no sooner have I finished a meal that I am looking for another?" She was speaking half in jest, the other in earnest, "But where is everybody?"

"Buzzy went off in search of his valet."

"Why would he do that?"

"I chanced to remark that I found the mode of his neckcloth hideous."

She laughed. "And he values your opinion so much that he must immediately attend to the matter."

"Precisely so. I am held to be quite a nonpareil in London, you know."

"Yes, and so you are, but what must you do but waste yourself on that dreadful girl!" said Lacey without thinking.

He was flattered by her remark. It surged through him and his eyes softened. "Ah, Lace... you are such an innocent. I am getting no better than I deserve. I am afraid Miss Rainbird and I shall suit well enough for our individual purposes."

"Oh, sir... does money mean that much?"

He smiled ruefully. "When you haven't it, yes, it does." He frowned. "And what of you? Aren't you planning on marrying Buzz? Wouldn't that further your own situation?"

"What a perfectly odious thing to think and an even worse thing to say!" she retorted hotly.

"You mean you aren't going to marry Buzz? If so, you shouldn't be leading him on with stolen kisses."

"If you keep speaking along such lines I shall be excessively put out with you!"

"Then you are going to marry him?" he persisted.

She cocked her head. What would she have him think? Better to be vague. "I haven't decided."

"He is quite a catch, you know." He was baiting her.

"That doesn't signify," she returned, not falling for it.

"What does then?"

"I told you once before."

"Ah, yes, Love. It is nonsense," he said quietly.

"Then you would have me marry Buzz?" This time she was baiting.

"I would have you happy," he returned.

She stomped her foot, which astonished him, but they were not allowed any further conversation alone as Lady Bussingham came fluttering in and on either side of her was Lady Carmen Stanhope and Lord Douglas Collymore. Lacey lost all color in her cheeks and thought surely now she was undone!

Trouble, trouble, trouble! What to do? What would Aunt Jana do? How would she handle the introductions? She had had a long woman-to-woman talk with Lady Bussingham about Lord Collymore and knew that her ladyship understood her situation. She could trust her but there was the problem of Lady Stanhope. She would have to be introduced to Lady Stanhope. Drat!

Lady Bussingham was attempting a cheery face. "Lace, dear, I know I needn't make Lord Collymore known to you, for you are quite good friends; however, I should like you to meet his aunt, Lady Carmen Stanhope."

Lace made a slight curtsy and felt the color flood back into her cheeks as she heard Lady Stanhope say,

"Did you say Lace?" Lady Stanhope felt as though Jana Bussingham was handling the introductions far too speedily for decorum. She didn't like that. "What a very odd name, to be sure. Well, then, I understand you are quite a favorite about the Bussingham household, but I didn't catch your full name, my dear...?"

"Eden," put in Lady Bussingham, pinching Lord Collymore's small pinky as she whizzed by toward the bellpull. "I shall ring for tea so that we may be comfortable."

Lord Collymore's brow was up. Lace here? He should have realized, of course, because her friendship with the Bussingham's was well known to him, but what was this? Lace calling herself by her mother's maiden name? What was happening here? He moved forward and took up both of Lace's hands. "Lace! This is a surprise." Then in an aside for her ears alone, "You little hell kitten, your stepmama is pulling her hair out over you!"

She looked directly into his dark gray eyes and wondered what it was that she had found so fascinating there. "I daresay it has done her some good," she whispered back tongue in cheek.

He had the urge to touch her nose. It was always so when he was near her. She was so alive, so refreshing. He was not in love with her but very willing to be. "We shall have to talk, you and I."

Sir Roland watched them as they made their quiet exchanges, nodding absently as he was introduced to the dowager Stanhope. Collymore was a gambling acquaintance of his and he had enjoyed a convivial evening or two in that gentleman's company but the man was a rake, very much like himself, and he wasn't pleased to see him on such intimate terms with Lace. Damn! Was there no end to her suitors? Balloonists, Buzzy and now Collymore? He wished he could edge up closer and hear what it was that kept the two of them in such close conversation.

"My lord..." whispered Lacey to Collymore, "I do agree, we must have a private conversation..."

"Indeed Miss *Eden*," said Collymore looking at her intensely, "I would be delighted."

Sir Roland had disengaged himself from Lady Stanhope and crossed the room in time to hear this last. Darker grew his frown. He extended his hand. "Good to see you, Collymore, but whatever brings you into Nottingham?"

Collymore shook Roland's hand warmly. "What brings me, old fellow, is pretty much what brought you."

"Really? Things tight with you?"

"Deadly old man, deadly . . . but I expect they shall get better," he said, smiling down at Lace in a familiar fashion.

What was he up to? Devil! Why was he looking at Lace in that manner? What good could it do for him to engage Lace's affection? She was penniless. Did he mean to trifle with her? Devil take him if he tried it, for Sir Roland vowed to have his head for the effort.

Lacey's eyes lit up with a sudden inspiration, "Oh, Collymore, as it happens it is famous good luck that you have come. My gelding is having trouble with his left fore leg. I can't find any heat in the legs and suspect he has injured something in his shoulder. You have ever had a way with such things. Come with me to the stables."

"An excellent notion," agreed Lady Bussingham, surprising Sir Roland no little bit for the lackey had just arrived with the tea tray.

"Come on, then," said Lacey digging her hand into Collymore's and turning to the company and saying sweetly, "Please do excuse us, we shall only be a few moments."

Collymore was pulled along all the while wondering what it was she was up to but pleased as could be to find he was at last playing an important role in her cogitations.

Chapter Nine

LORD COLLYMORE WAITED only for the butler to close the front door at their backs before he took up Lace's arm and urged her to look up at him. "Now, Lace, what is all this? Why the masquerade?"

She had been thinking furiously all this while and there was but one answer that would serve to silence Collymore. Obviously he was still interested in promoting a marriage of convenience with her. Hence, she concluded, he would not at this hour appreciate any competition, especially a rival of Sir Roland's stamp. She put on a face to match her tale.

"Collymore, you would never credit it, but Sir Roland is a fortune hunter!" said she in shocked accents.

"Is he?" returned his lordship cautiously, wondering what this was leading up to. "What makes you think so?"

"He told me so," she returned honestly. "At least...he told me he intends to make a match of convenience because he hasn't a sou to his name."

"Did he, by God?" exclaimed Collymore momentarily diverted, and then frowning because the issue at hand had been sidestepped and dusted. "But Lace...that does not explain anything."

"Doesn't it? Well, then, how shall I start?" She meant to confuse the issue. "Well, I had better start with the highwaymen..."

"Bridle-culls? What have you to do with bridle-culls?" ejaculated his lordship, his eyes growing wider still.

"Nothing at all, thanks to Sir Roland. You see...I was on the road, riding Cricket, when I was set upon. Sir Roland happened at that moment and rescued me..."

"How fortunate for Sir Roland..." said his lordship dryly, thinking that Roland now had the advantage over him.

She ignored this and continued her story, using her hands graphically all the while. "So, there I was with Sir Roland...and he saw in a flash that I wasn't a boy..."

"A boy? Why would he think you were a boy?" Lord Collymore was beginning to feel confused.

"My clothes. I was disguised as a boy. I thought it would better serve at that hour of night...but don't interrupt anymore, Colly, for I shall grow impatient and not tell you the whole!" she commanded, and then quickly before he could reply to this, "...So there I was, with Sir Roland insisting that he must offer me his protection. I had to think quite quickly, you know. Couldn't very well tell him I was Lacey

Burton, heiress. No...he seemed a bit of a rake, you see, and I thought he might prove untrustworthy and use that bit of knowledge to his advantage. I was in a sticky situation, wasn't I?"

"I'll say. Egad, Lace, that was pretty plunging in the wind...but..."

"Shh...I am not finished. Now where was I? Oh, yes, in Sir Roland's coach. We discovered a common bond, Bussingham! We were both headed for Bussingham. I told him my name was Eden and that I was a penniless girl running away from a marriage with an old groat..."

Collymore brought up Lacey's hand to his lips and his tone held a special note, quiet, reproachful. "Why did you run away, Lace?"

She blushed. "I would liefer by far not discuss that with you, Colly...let us just say my stepmama made it impossible for me to stay."

"It would help me to know what she did to make you go? It would help if I knew whether I was to blame," he said taking the initiative.

"Please, Colly...we were friends once. I should like to believe you had nought to do with my stepmother's schemes, but I know better and therefore warn you now to drop the subject." She put up her hand. "Do you wish to hear the end of my confession or not?"

He grinned. "Yes, kitten, do tell me all."

"So we traveled to Bussingham together. I was disguised as a boy and luckily we went unnoticed. I have convinced the viscount and his mother to introduce me as Miss Lace Eden because I do not wish my stepmother to find me and because I do not want Sir Roland to know I am an heiress. It would make things very difficult."

"He will one day discover the truth, you know. Sir

Roland is accounted by many to be omniscient."

"Yes, but by then he will have been married to Miss Rainbird and therefore no longer in a position to force me to marry him because of my indiscretion."

Lord Collymore's brain was fast at work. Lace was falling into his hands. He could send word to Daphne, have her travel to Nottingham and ... but that would not look well with the viscount and his mother as witnesses. No, he would have to woo the chit and with Daphne out of the way, he would now have a much better opportunity. Sir Roland might find Lace's face and figure delightful but Sir Roland would not seduce an innocent maid, not if she were penniless. Yes, this story of Lace's suited him very well indeed.

There was but one other rival Collymore could think of and that was the viscount. "Of course I shan't give you away ... but tell me what does our friend Buzz think of all this?"

"Oh, you know Buzzy. He is in a miff over the entire affair. He thinks I was imprudent to travel alone; he thinks I was far more imprudent to travel with Roland and he thinks I am a bedlamite for persisting in my course but he would not give me away. He is not such a pudding heart as to do that."

"I think our Buzz has a fondness for behaving the Grand Turk. Did he read you a lecture, kitten?"

She smiled, "'Twas no more than I deserved, for I suppose I did behave impulsively, but I could scarcely have done less ... such were my options." She looked away a moment. Here she was conversing with Collymore as though her heart had never fluttered at the sound of his approach, as though she had never longed for his kiss, for the touch of his hand. All that had flown. How had she ever thought he was her knight in shining armor? Yes, knights still existed but not so that you could see their shine.

They had by then reached the stables and he looked down at her quizzically. "Well, my kitten, shall we go in or circumvent it all for more pleasurable pursuits in the garden?" His hand moved deftly from her elbow to her hip.

She tilted away from his touch and took a few steps from him. She was not adverse to a few moments of dallying. It would serve him right to think he was making headway and then find himself out. It was just the sort of set down he needed, for he was still a lying cad.

"And what pursuits did you have in mind, my lord?" she said coyly.

This was a new Lace. A devilishly mature and bewitching creature. Gone was the schoolgirl air and missish blushes and in its place a woman whose eyes engaged, whose lips taunted, whose figure mesmerized. He moved closer to her and made a successful grab for her waist. "Shall I show you, kitten ... ?" He had her very nearly in position for this when suddenly his arms were empty. Slippery chit, he thought, feeling his blood rise. She was exciting him to further devilry. He came after her slowly, his smile warm, hungry. "You play an interesting game, love."

Lace looked toward the house. It was time to return and she would have moved in its direction had she not seen a very determined Sir Roland coming toward them. She pretended not to see him as she stood her ground and allowed Collymore's approach to bring them closer together. "'Tis no game, my lord," she said, the tease light in her lovely voice.

Sir Roland could only see Lacey's profile and it quite set up his bristles. Was this the amusing child he had rescued and brought to Bussingham? What had happened to Lace Eden? She was a woman and yet there was still so much of the child about her. She was an innocent, she was like a pretty young bird spreading its wings, testing its strength. This afternoon, finding her in the viscount's arms had sent bubbling blood coursing through him. Why? Because she had set him in an avuncular light did he also cast himself in such a role? No! He felt the pangs of jealousy. Why? He didn't know, didn't want to know. He had to ignore such sensations.

If he were to survive, he had to ignore all such emotions. He had to proceed with his plans and marry Letty Rainbird. But here was Collymore and he had the look of the stud about him as he pranced around Lace. Roland didn't like that. Collymore could hurt Lace...and then he saw Lace move seductively to Collymore's play! Damn, but his fists itched to land the fellow a blow. He wouldn't have it. He wouldn't have anyone touch Lace in that familiar way, but hold, what are you at? You haven't the right.

He was upon them, conflicting sensations raging against logic nearly expressed on his countenance, but his voice was controlled yet clipped as he said, "I am sent to tell you to hurry back for Lady Bussingham has sent for another pot of hot tea." He hesitated, and then quietly, "However, if my message is ill timed, and I can see that it is, I can return to her ladyship with the message that Cricket needs your attention." He was looking at Lace now.

He was angry. Was he jealous? She smiled sweetly at him, ignoring his mood and his innuendo. "Oh, no, we are all done, are we not, my lord?" She turned to Collymore.

"We are whatever you please, love," he answered gallantly, and went to take up her elbow.

Instead, she slinked her hand through Sir Roland's, turned and took up Collymore's arm as well. This was heaven, or very near it for a girl out of the schoolroom!

Morning! It came in strong with its spring scents filling the breeze and wafting 'round Lace's sleepy head until she blinked her eyes open. Get up, slug-a-bed, she told herself. There are things to be done. Oh, but it was so nice lying there recalling the previous evening. Collymore and Lady Stanhope had stayed to dinner and what a lively meal that had been!

The viscount had come in waving the *Times* and declaring that he didn't know what things were coming to when common thieves were allowed to abscond with their prizes not once, twice but three times, leaving nary a clue!

Everyone had crowded 'round him as he read off the article that took up most of the first page.

"Look...it all started with a small theft at Lady Darbough's ball..." he said, pointing.

"I was there that night!" shuddered Lady Stanhope.

"Hmm. Yes, I can still remember poor Claire screeching at the top of her lungs," agreed Lady Bussingham. "Snatched her diamonds right off her neck and was gone...in a flash!"

"Were you there too, Buzz?" asked Lace, wide-eyed.

"No...but Roland was," he said. "What exactly happened, Ro?"

Sir Roland appeared bored with the topic. "I can but vaguely recall the evening. It was something of a squeeze and noisier than most, I think."

Buzz pulled a face. "What about you, Collymore?"

"I? I believe I was in the...er...gardens at the actual moment of the theft. I came in afterward to find the house in an uproar and many of the guests departing. I did the same."

"I call that a piece of sadly wanting spirit," decreed Lace, eyeing him with disfavor. "The very least you could have done was to investigate."

He moved nearer to her. "But, Lace, I had no way of knowing it would be the beginning of a series of thefts and there were already too many hands in the dough. The very best I could do was to get out of the way and allow the professionals a go at it."

"I suppose..." she said doubtfully. "Well...read on, Buzz!"

He mumbled over the printed lines until he reached more pertinent facts. "Ah, yes, the next family to be hit was the Scarlingtons. True to fashion, it says here, the thieves hit whilst Lady Scarlington was hostessing a Venetian Breakfast." He looked up from the paper. "I was at that one. She didn't even realize her emeralds were gone until I mentioned it to her. Told her I was glad she removed them; emeralds in the morning seemed a bit much to me. Dreadful fright she gave me for what must she do but clutch her neck, scream in my face and fling herself at me saying she was going to swoon!"

Lace chuckled. "Oh, Buzz...the poor woman..."

"Poor woman? Zounds, Lace...she nearly took me down with her...would have too if Roland didn't put his shoulder into m'back! Saved the day with that one. Large woman, Lady Scarlington!"

Lace laughed. "Then Sir Roland was with you? But...then what happened?"

"It was a terrible affair. What with her husband in India...thank goodness Flora was with her," said Lady Stanhope.

"Flora? Flora Morely...was with Lady Scarlington? How was that?" asked Lace. She had refrained from asking the dowager why Flora had not come to tea. Instinct told her it had something to do with Collymore's presence.

The dowager loved being the center of attention and as Lace's question brought all eyes to focus on her she was pleased enough to answer. "Well, Flora had gone to Lady Scarlington after Flora's brother, Lord Davenport's dreadful accident..."

"Accident?" put in Lace. "I thought it was a duel...?"

"Just so, my dear," said the dowager, pleased to find Lace in possession of the facts. "Terrible thing. Awful for poor Flora what with her own problems to be faced with such a scandal...but I am digressing. When Lord Scarlington returned from India, he and his lady thought it might be better for Flora to find another post. I was most happy to provide that for her."

"How...good of you," murmured Lady Bussingham, doing the required.

Silently, Lacey thought how terrible life must have been treating her pretty friend Flora. A dull look came into her eyes. Sir Roland noted it and leaned toward her to touch her chin. He said while still looking at Lace, "Well, Buzz, do continue; what else does the paper tell us?" He already knew the answer, for he had been present during all three of the notable robberies, but he wanted Lace wide-eyed once more.

"I fancy we all remember that last at the Duke of Winthrop's masquerade," said Buzz grimly. "It was the first time the villains broke their pattern. Poor Elizabeth."

"But...what did they do?" exclaimed Lace.

"Bludgeoned her!" retorted Lady Bussingham,

shuddering over the memory. The Duchess of Winthrop was one of her favorite ladies of fashion. "Such fiends they must be to strike a frail slip of a woman. Her health has not been right since."

"But why did they do it? What made them do such a thing?" asked Lace.

"I fancy the duchess must have tried to resist," answered Collymore.

"Well, good for her!" returned Lace. Here now was a woman to be admired. Why, the very idea of all these women being victims without even realizing it until the act was done was incredible.

Sir Roland's eyes twinkled. "One must keep in mind that all she won for her show of spirit was a lump on the head."

"Yes, sir, but she went down fighting. *She tried!* Failing doesn't signify if one knows that he or she has tried," argued Lace.

"Failing always counts, more so if a great deal of effort went into the thing, my minx," he answered.

She had no logic to answer him with but she had a store of feelings. "I would still admire the one who tries."

His eyes stroked her. "And I admire only you, little one." His voice was low, his tone holding a meaning that thrilled her.

She was not totally surprised by his words. She had felt something of what he was thinking. She had seen there lurking in his eyes something of what he felt for her and she knew her answer was ill timed, but she could not stop herself, and the words came out.

"And yet you are courting Letty Rainbird."

He grew stiff. "Yes, and I *am* courting Letty Rainbird. That is the difference between your fancies and the world's realities."

She turned away from him. "Collymore...were

you at the duchess's masquerade too? Did you see anything?"

"We were all there; none of us saw a thing. Not a blasted thing," he answered in some disgust.

"If the duchess put up some resistance...did she get a look at the man?"

"Not a look, not a sense of size...in fact, we still don't know if there was one thief, two thieves...whether they are men, what accomplices they might have. We have absolutely nothing to go on. The duchess never saw her assailant. She felt a hand at her throat and made a fist with which to curb his effort. A hand went over her mouth from behind and then a heavy object put her out. She awoke to find her husband waving her fan over her face and the family jewels gone from her ears and throat," recited Buzz.

"But that is terrible. How can they get in and out without being noticed. Surely such ruffians must stand out? How do they pass as invited guests?" exclaimed Lacey.

"That is the crux of it, Lace," he returned. He set the paper aside and made a pyramid of his hands shading his mouth. "A problem indeed. He didn't stand out among us as an outsider and therefore I have but one conclusion to offer."

"Which is?" said Sir Roland, his tone curious.

"That he was an invited guest," said Buzz dramatically.

"But that is impossible," returned his mother. "All the guests were of the ton...I don't remember mention of there being any skirters. Why, Peter...you are saying that a friend has done this?"

"I am," he insisted.

"But, my lord," said the dowager Stanhope, "I think that highly improbable."

He sighed, "Who, then?"

"Who, indeed?" said Sir Roland. "Buzz has a very intriguing point to ponder here."

"Oh, my!" breathed Lace. "But this is awful. What has the paper to say about it all?"

"Only that in the last two weeks no other thefts of that nature have taken place, leaving investigators to believe that the thief or thieves are now laying low."

"But what of the jewels? I should imagine such notable pieces would be hard to sell," said Jana Bussingham.

"None of them have turned up in any form. Odd that, but perhaps the thief has the sense to hold onto them for a time," answered her son.

"Or perhaps he means to strike again," said Collymore on an ominous note.

Sir Roland listened to this but said nothing of what he thought. He turned instead to Lace and applied himself to catch her again in conversation but no, he was courting Letty Rainbird. So it was. He excused himself and rode into town to the local inn to forget his troubles.

Lacey was left with a gentleman on either side of her, both attempting almost successfully to please while her mind wandered after Sir Roland. What could she do? How could she stop him from making the mistake without telling him she was herself an heiress? Enough!

She got up from the bed and put her musings aside. It was a new day. Her mother had always tucked her in at night, saying sweetly, "Tomorrow is a new day, make of it what you will." Well, that was exactly what she would do!

Chapter Ten

LETTY RAINBIRD PUT a lavender kid-gloved hand to her chest and felt the rapid pulse of her heartbeat through the heavy material of her violet riding habit. She shouldn't be doing this! It would only cause her more pain. Wasn't she done with such emotions? Hadn't he hurt her enough already? Would that last scene with him in London never be stilled, vanquished, obliterated? Would it always repeat itself in her mind's scope? As though for answer she dug her heel into her horse's flank and bounded forward.

She had to go! The words he had written were vividly alive. She had shredded his letter, fed the tattered pages to the fire but over and over his words urged her on. "I worship you still, Letty. Please come to me." She wanted him to prove the words true.

She wanted to believe. Perhaps it would then erase the haunting nightmare...perhaps. But no logic sent her across the fields to Charles Teggs! Logic rarely plays a role in such doings.

She could see his balloon there in the distance. Fool! she berated herself. You are taking a chance. You have a titled nobleman paying you court. Sir Roland is both handsome and witty. Sir Roland is a Corinthian. Sir Roland is exciting...yet it is Charles Teggs who draws you. Fool!

Charles saw her coming and put down his tools. It was a clear, warm, spring day made for his plan but it would take a sight more than that to win Letty Rainbird again. He had done it once but a stupid mistake had cost him her fortune. Damn, how could he have expected her to come barging in on him? Then he had thought her lady enough to stay away from his bachelor lodgings. But here she was now and that was certainly a small victory. He put up his hand and went toward her as she slowed her horse.

"Letty..." His hands were already at her waist lifting her down, pressing her close to his firm body.

He had the power to take her breath from her. She felt as though the world were swimming 'round her eyes. She had to stop this sensation. She pulled away and her tone was confused. He was reducing her to the green girl she had been then, the girl she thought she would never be again. "I...I don't know why I came..."

"You know why, darling. This year has cost us both dearly." He was taking hold of her again. "Letty...I have suffered without you. When I saw you yesterday I thought I would burst. Have you the heart to forgive me my sin against you? Letty, that egregious day hurt us both...Letty look at me."

An agonized sound emitted from her pouting

mouth and she looked away but he turned her face roughly in his hand. "Answer me, Letty!"

"You want me to forgive you? Very well, then, you have it, my forgiveness. Surely I was nought but a young fool to think you could be faithful whilst courting me?"

"Stop it!" He shook her. "What did you think me? A monk? Yes, I courted you, wanted you, loved you and I love you now... but, Letty, I could not take you... not till our wedding day. She was nothing to me. Nothing! A physical release, for Letty you had me in heat. Do you understand what I am telling you? She was nothing." His mouth had already sought and found her own, his lips had already parted hers, his hands were already lowering her to the grass.

"Stop... Charles... stop..." She pushed ineffectually at his chest.

"Do you want me to stop? Really, Letty... do you?"

"Yes! I am going to marry Sir Roland," she said on a hard note.

He pulled himself up. "Marry Sir Roland? The man you were with yesterday afternoon?"

"Yes... at least... he hasn't asked me yet, but I think he shall and I am going to say yes."

He stood up and took her hand so that she too was standing but very near. "Well, then, my love, we have nothing left to discuss, you and I. You are neatly sealing both our fates."

She wanted to answer this but he turned abruptly away from her and returned to the rigging 'round his balloon. She wanted to rail at him, tell him what she thought of him. Why didn't he beg her not to marry Sir Roland? Why? She stamped her foot and returned to her grazing horse.

Once mounted she pulled sharply on the reins, turning her horse about and galloping off toward home. He turned to watch her retreat and smiled to himself. She cared. Yes, she cared a great deal more than she would have him know... and if this proved false, and she really did marry this Sir Roland, no matter, he had other means to see him to luxury!

Sir Roland watched Lacey cross the central hall from the shadows of the great stairs. He should let her pass. Don't stop her. He took a step forward. "Lace...?"

She turned and illuminated his face with her smile. "Sir Roland? I thought I was the only one abroad at this hour."

He appraised her quizzically. "Yet you have on there a riding habit to rival the London belles."

Laughing, she conceded him the point and then with her arms out at her sides she did a graceful twirl. "It is nice, isn't it?"

He thought the olive green ensemble with its black frogging was certainly cut by a practiced and expensive hand. He wondered at Lady Bussingham's generosity. There was, of course, but one conclusion and that was her ladyship must be fairly certain Lace was about to become her daughter-in-law. 'Tis interesting to see how one can easily fit facts to circumstances and come up with a fantasy that is most realistic. At any rate his conclusion bothered him into a frown.

"Too lovely to go unseen, brat."

"Then I am quite pleased you are up and about, for now I have been seen." She moved boldly toward him, her face tilted up to look full into those marvelously gold-specked eyes. "Your compliments, sir, are all I seek..."

He flicked her nose with his finger. "Innocent, you don't know with what you play," he said softly. He had to set her aside, he had to escape her face, her eyes, her tantalizing movements. "Go about your business before you get us both into trouble."

"But I want to get us into trouble. It would be a sight better than letting you marry Letty Rainbird."

He put up a warning brow. "Off with you, minx."

She pulled a face but turned and did his bidding. He stood looking at the empty hall long after she was gone. What was happening to him? What was it about Lace that so made him feel? How would he rid himself of these very annoying sensations? What right had they to intrude now when he was about to propose to another woman?

Lacey's preoccupation with Sir Roland diverted her attention from the road. Unwittingly, she found herself nearing the field that would take her to Charles Teggs and his balloon. However, just as she was struggling with the decision to continue or turn back a very harassed young woman rode up sharp and short of the gate.

"Confound it all!" seethed Letty Rainbird. "Someone has closed the gate!" She looked about for help and saw a familiar young woman on the road. Lace Eden. What was Miss Eden doing in this vicinity? She had seen Lace with Charles yesterday but had not given it much thought. Now here she was again? Irritating, yet she managed a smile, "Hallo! Miss Eden," she called.

Lace went into a sitting trot and came up to the gate. "Good morning, Miss Rainbird, how nice to see you. I am so pleased to see I am not alone in my love for early-morning equitation."

"What? Oh...oh, yes, I enjoy a ride at this hour...now and then...but as you can see someone has latched the gate and I daren't jump it with that ditch on the other side."

Lace's brow went up. For any other she would have gladly offered to jump down herself and unlock the gate but she didn't like Letty's hinting. It set up her bristles. "What is the problem?" she asked innocently.

Letty heaved a sigh. "I do so hate having to dismount in the field. I am bound to get my boots wet to say nothing of my new habit."

"A pity that," said Lace.

Letty's cheeks flushed with anger; after all this chit was her junior. The very least she could do would be to try and bend over and unlatch the gate, so she said as much.

"But, Miss Rainbird, you are forgetting...I have the ditch to contend with."

"You are being very uncooperative," complained Miss Rainbird.

"Am I? Perhaps you are expecting too much," returned Lace uncompromisingly. She could be stubborn at times, and this was one of those times, yet she tried to overcome it. You are being jealous and spiteful, Lacey Burton, she told herself. Now, be nice! She relented. "But never mind, Miss Rainbird...if you can't manage the thing, I shall contrive to do it for you."

It was at this moment that the farmer who had perpetrated the problem at hand returned to the scene of the crime. Scratching his head he jogged over, mumbling something incoherent as he opened the gate wide. Miss Rainbird guided her horse past without thanking the man, so Lacey did it for her. Letty Rainbird waited in the road for Lace to catch up and then turned her ice-cold gray eyes upon her.

"You didn't have to thank him for me, Miss Eden! If I thought he deserved gratitude I would have given it to him. He had no right closing the gate to begin with."

"I was taught to think and behave differently, Miss Rainbird," returned Lace, throwing a rope over her growing temper.

Letty said nothing to this but cropped her horse meanly on his rump and bounded forward. Lace clicked her tongue and accomplished the same. Riding abreast in a controlled canter, Lace called, "Why do you use a crop, Miss Rainbird? Surely your horse isn't a slug?"

"It accomplishes what I want," answered Miss Rainbird coldly.

"Does it? I should think you might learn other measures to obtain the desired effects without the constant use of a crop. After all, your horse will learn to respond to the signals you give him."

Letty Rainbird had had enough! Her morning was proving to be beyond her control, and in a fit of temper she brought her crop down again, but this time she brought it down on Cricket's rump.

Lace's black gelding had never been cropped before. It was both startling and painful. He screeched with fear, bucked, pulled on his reins, which Lace had been holding loosely, and bounded forward wildly out of control!

Sir Roland had taken to horse soon after Lacey had left the grounds. He was crossing the fields urging his bay gelding onward as he followed Lace's signs. Why? Why did he want to continue a line of conversation with her that was more dangerous than anything else? No answer. He had no answer; he only knew that after her departure he felt strangely restless. He crossed the backwoods road and came to a fork and stopped his horse as he strove to make his decision. There, two female riders were coming toward him. He was just out of their view but he had them well in sight. Letty and Lace...together? And then he saw Letty's upraised arm, saw her bring it down hard and instinctively put out a hand as though to stop her. Damn! Lace's horse shot out from under her and ran frenzied toward the woods. Damn! Then he took off after her, his heart in his throat throbbing desperately as he galloped headlong toward his goal.

Cricket was not responding! What to do? Don't panic, she told herself; lean back, lean back ...back...pull from the shoulders! But it wasn't working. Cricket's mouth was numb and he was intent on escaping from that which frightened him. Lacey called to him, she used her reins, easing them and then pulling them in again, gripping with her knees, leaning back into her saddle, and then in a last-ditch effort before they hit the narrow path in the woods, she yelled sharply, angrily.

"Stop it, boy! Cricket, do you hear me? Stop it! Whoa!" Simultaneously she yanked hard, quickly with an up and then a down motion on one rein.

It worked. Something clicked in the horse's mind. Pain...there was a painful discomfort in his mouth. His mistress had yanked on his mouth. He was misbehaving, disobeying her command. She wanted him to stop. He heard her voice, understood her tone; she was angry. There was authority to her words. He slowed, snorted with a vigorous shake of his head and then stopped. He stood, blowing out air, digging the earth with his hoof, snorting, still somewhat frenzied by his ordeal and then he heard her voice again. There was a security in the sound. His ears went forward to her soothing.

"There now, Cricket...there...you are all right," Lacey was saying, though her heart was beating wildly and her eyes were still wide with her own fright.

"Lace!" it was Sir Roland; she was all right. He could see that she was shaken, but thank God, she was all right. He controlled a sudden urge to jump off his horse and pull her into the safety of his arms. It wouldn't do. Letty was most certainly at his back.

Lace saw him. He was here. No knight in shining armor, but so very close to it that she nearly heard the accompaniment of music to his approach. She needed him and he was here. She could see the concern on his face. He cared. She just knew he cared.

"Sir Roland..." she breathed. She couldn't say more. It had been a frightening experience. She was out of breath, shaky from the episode, all too aware how very close she had come to finding both her horse and herself badly injured, but above all these considerations her anger mounted. She saw Letty coming up on her horse and suddenly Lace was off Cricket and striding hard in Letty's direction. Lace hadn't bothered to secure Cricket and he wandered off a space before Sir Roland had his reins and looked up to see Lace making a hard line for Letty. His brow went up and he felt no little anxiety for Letty's immediate future.

Letty stopped her horse and a horrified expression came to her countenance as she watched Lace's progress. Letty's hand came up to ward off Lace's onslaught for surely Lace gave every appearance of a mad tigress about to strike. However, instead of finding herself brutally attacked she felt the crop pulled out of her grip and sat in astonishment as Lace broke the thing over her upraised knee.

As the crop splintered and Lace flung the offending article to the brush, Lace's voice came low and disdainfully. "Manners forbid my telling you in front of Sir Roland just exactly what I think of you and your behavior." With this she turned and went once more to Cricket, thanking Sir Roland for holding his reins and mounting nimbly and gracefully into her saddle.

"Lace ... wait ..." called Sir Roland, for she moved her horse 'round to leave them.

She turned to face him and could see the admiration in his eyes, and her resolve to leave him with his hateful intended softened. "Yes, Sir Roland, what is it?"

"My dear child, you can't mean to ride home alone after such an ordeal?"

"But why not? I fancy I should be a great deal safer without Miss Rainbird at my side."

"Nevertheless, I will see you home," he said firmly. Letty was blushing furiously but she well deserved that hit.

"There is no need, Sir Roland. I am certain you will want to escort Miss Rainbird to her home. She is, after all, somewhat farther adrift from it than I am from Bussingham."

"Your suggestion exhibits that you never lack in sense, Miss Eden," he said formally. "Therefore, it should appear reasonable that both Miss Rainbird and I shall accompany you to Bussingham where we may refresh ourselves, after which I shall be most pleased to see Miss Rainbird home." Without waiting for Lace's reply he turned to Miss Rainbird. "Does my plan meet with your approval, Miss Rainbird?"

"Yes, of course," answered the girl attempting sangfroid. There was only one way out of this very embarrassing situation and that was to display no regret, no shame.

Lace breathed a sound of disbelief not unmixed with exasperation. "Oh, capital, Sir Roland!" with which she bounded forward taking the lead.

Chapter Eleven

LACE'S MOOD WAS one of disquiet as she watched Letty flirt outrageously with Sir Roland. Letty's laugh pierced her sharply and she suddenly could stand it no more. She excused herself politely and moved toward the library doors. Sir Roland frowned and had a strong inclination to follow but held himself in check.

Lacey closed the door at her back and stood a moment to catch a long whiff of air. Oh, it was the outside of enough! How could he marry that wench? How could he? She looked up to see Buckles coming toward her, a card on his silver tray, and with some curiosity she looked past him to find a small, plump man fidgeting in the hall. Upon further inspection she received the clear image of a man who held a clerical occupation, for such was his manner and dress.

"Who is that man, Buckles?" she asked softly as the butler approached.

"A Mr. Farnsborough to see Sir Roland, Miss," said the butler, his hand going to the door latch.

"Wait...Buckles...no one is supposed to know that Sir Roland is here at Bussingham. What does the man want?"

"He didn't say, Miss."

"Very well, show him into the study. I will see him, as Sir Roland is engaged at the moment."

"As you wish, Miss Lace," returned Buckles. He too thought that Mr. Farnsborough had the look of clerk. It was known among the servants that Sir Roland was escaping dunning collectors and therefore he agreed with Miss Eden that Sir Roland should not be disturbed.

"One more thing, Buckles...did you say that Sir Roland was at home?"

"Sir Roland had instructed me to avoid indicating anything one way or the other on that question. I advised Mr. Farnsborough that I would take his card to my lady, who might know the whereabouts of Sir Roland."

"Excellent, Buckles. You are a good fellow...now go show him into the study. I will see him there," she said, bouncing across the floor to the study doors.

She had scarcely a moment to compose herself before the doors opened and Mr. Farnsborough walked into the room. She nodded and graciously invited him to be seated. He sighed and took up the invitation.

"This is most disappointing, Miss Eden..." said the gentleman. "I made certain I would find Sir Roland here..."

"Did you? How so?" she asked, her brow going up.

"Well, you must know that it was Sir Roland's man in London who put me in his way..."

"Did he? How much did you pay him to betray his employer?" snapped Lace, incensed with this piece of disloyalty.

"Pay him? Betray...? I...don't understand..."

"Don't you? Tell me, Mr. Farnsborough, do you always go this far to dun a man?"

"Dun...? Oh, dear, no, no. I am not trying to collect tradesmen bills. My, my...quite the opposite, Miss Eden, quite the opposite."

She sat up and looked long at him. "I don't understand."

"As you may have already noted from my card, I am here representing my firm, Longworth & Son...barristers at law, hired in this instance to locate Sir Roland for the purpose of presenting documents requiring his signature..."

"I still don't understand..."

"Miss Eden, Sir Roland has come into a respectable inheritance!"

"Oh...how dreadful..." was her immediate response.

Mr. Farnsborough put on a shocked expression. "Dreadful...? I don't see that...I mean 'tis not a fortune, but most respectable, I do assure you..."

"But, who has died, sir?"

"Oh, I see now what it is. No, no...I was given to understand that Sir Roland was scarcely acquainted with the fellow. A cousin of sorts...the estates come to Sir Roland through an old entailment as the deceased had no surviving relatives."

Lacey Eden did a remarkable thing for a woman in her position. She swore beneath her breath, "Confound it! This ruins everything."

"Really, Miss Eden, I don't understand..."

Lace got to her feet and proceeded to pace, hands clasped at her waist. Inheritance. Now, he would not have to marry Letty Rainbird. But, but... oh, dear, it was for the wrong reason. She wanted Sir Roland to come to her in spite of his difficulties. She wanted him to say, "hang my poverty... I can marry no one but you, Lace..." This inheritance would shatter that ideal! No realist was Lace. "Mr. Farnsborough... I regret to advise you that Sir Roland has left for Northumberland early this morning. We do not expect him here again for three weeks..." She would give herself that time limit. If she had not won him over by then, so be it, she would then allow the fates their way.

"Oh, dear... oh, dear... his accounts will not be set in order until I can return these documents duly signed to the bank!" said Mr. Farnsborough, diving into his leather-bound satchel and waving the papers at Miss Eden in some agitation. "I suppose this will mean another trip for me. I did so hope he would be here..."

"Mr. Farnsborough, there is not the least need for you to follow Sir Roland into Northumberland. Besides, it would be useless. He is on a jaunt with friends and there is no saying where their exact heading will be. Why don't you leave the papers with me? I shall put them into her ladyship's care and together we will sit Sir Roland down as soon as he returns and post them to you thereafter."

This sounded reasonable to Mr. Farnsborough. He had friends he dearly wished to spend the weekend with in the area and Miss Eden's solution came as the only answer. "Very well, Miss Eden, I shall leave these with you..." he said, placing the papers on the stained-wood coffee table.

She picked them up. "May I offer you some

refreshment before you go?" asked Lace, dearly hoping he would decline the offer and go away before Sir Roland came in upon them.

"No, no thank you. I am promised to friends not far from here. Good-day to you Miss Eden," he said, rising to make her a bow.

She saw him to the front door, watched his departure from the hall window overlooking the drive, breathed a sigh of relief and turned to find Sir Roland with Letty on his arm coming her way.

She clutched the documents in her hand, smiled sweetly and said as she stepped forward, "Off so soon, Letty? Well...enjoy your ride home." With which she swept past, totally avoiding Sir Roland's inquiring eye.

Shortly afterward Lace was pacing in her room. It was still some minutes before noon, and as she was quite certain Letty's parents would invite Sir Roland to lunch with them, she had little hope of seeing him again until late afternoon. What to do in the meantime? How to plan his fall? She couldn't think. Her head needed clearing. A ride? Not now...at least not without purpose. Perhaps she would ride over to visit Flora...but then she risked an encounter with Collymore. Confound it all! She would take Buzzy!

With this decision neatly in hand she left her room and stalked the viscount, whom she finally found just coming in from the stables. "Oh, there you are, Buzz! I have been searching for you..."

"Have you?" He smiled wide. "Good. So, you missed me."

"Not exactly, but your mama has gone out for the morning and with Sir Roland off with Letty I was getting quite blue, but now you are here and you may escort me to the Stanhope Estate."

He was put out with her answer. She was making it

extremely difficult to be romantic, so he pulled a face. "I have only just come in and rather thought I'd like to sit down to a comfortable lunch."

"If I know you, you had a comfortable breakfast of sirloin and eggs. It won't do to eat lunch as well. You'll get fat. Come with me instead."

"Really, Lace..."

"Oh, please, Buzz...I don't want to ride over there alone. Not with Collymore lurking about."

He agreed with this wholeheartedly, "Yes, that's another thing, why do you want to ride over there when you know he might come down upon you?"

"I want to visit with Flora..."

"In that case, I certainly shall not allow it!" he said austerely. "'Tis time you stayed close to the house and relaxed a bit. You are the most restless female I have ever known."

"You won't allow it? In that case, my lord, I bid you a pleasant afternoon..." she said, giving him her back and making for the front door.

"Lace...I...oh, the devil! Very well, then, I'll accompany you," he said coming up to take her arm.

"How good you are," said Lace in a small voice.

He glanced at her sharply, for there was ever a hint of laughter in her voice. The girl was simply incorrigible!

Some twenty minutes later found their horses being watered in the Stanhope stables and the two young people being shown in by the Stanhope butler.

"Lady Stanhope is out this afternoon, My Lord..." offered the butler with just the proper quantity of regret in his tone.

"That doesn't matter..." put in Lacey before the viscount could respond. "It is Miss Morely we wish to see."

The butler's thin brow went up. Clearly he didn't

approve of such things. After all, whatever background Miss Morely had, she now worked for her living and therefore should not be hobnobbing with the quality. However, it was not his place to show the gentry theirs! "Won't you step into the parlor. I shall send word to Miss Morely immediately."

The viscount took up Lace's arm and led her through the open doorway into an elegantly furnished room and the first thing she noticed was a dark man with greased hair bending over a silver object. "What is that you are doing?" demanded Lacey at once, for there was something about the man that set up her bristles.

The man spun 'round and there was fear in the recesses of his eyes. "Nought...I be doing nought, Miss...this 'ere, it fell over when I was polishing the table...I was just putting it back," he said, waving a solid silver paperweight in the shape of a sea nymph at her.

The viscount was not totally satisfied. "What is your name, sir?"

"Stills...I'm her ladyship's footman...that's all...I'll be getting out of your way," he said, inching toward the door. The viscount took no action to stop him since, after all, everything was in order, but Lace watched the man beneath a frown. However, there were other matters at hand to occupy her mind and she soon dismissed him. There was no fire going in the grate and unconsciously she shivered. The viscount noticed this at once and went to repair the oversight by setting up kindling wood. It was from here that he worked until Flora arrived.

"Lace...how very sweet of you to come..." said Miss Morely, going forward, her hands extended.

The viscount's interest was arrested by the musical lilt of her voice and he looked up and stopped short his work. Why ... she was lovely ... angelic ...

There was something of the goddess in her mien as she stood in quiet grace. Her complexion was pale and framed by her flaxen silk waves of hair. The expression of sweetness in her blue eyes was gentle and the viscount found himself momentarily arrested by her appearance. Lacey made the introductions, and he discovered that his voice came out low and somewhat hoarse. He took up Flora's hand, put it to his lips and felt as though he moved in a dream.

Lacey watched him a moment in amused wonder until she caught the expression on Flora's face. Well, well, she thought, her brow going up, *what have we here?*

Chapter Twelve

OUTSIDE, THE DAY had turned balmy, the sky seemed to hold heavy promise of rain; inside, a fire burned in the Bussingham library grate. Lace's brown-print skirt rustled as she paced to and fro, arms folded into one another.

Lady Bussingham looked up from her letter-writing to catch the frenzy of Lace's movements and watched her a moment before putting down her quill. "Lace, dear, whatever has you in such a fidget?"

"'Tis nought. Just the day, I suppose. I'm restless..." said Lace, hoping to put her off.

"Really?" Lady Bussingham got to her elegantly shod feet and moved toward the sofa. "Come over here, love, and tell me what really has you up in the boughs and ready to jump?"

Lace stopped and let go a sigh. She eyed Jana Bussingham speculatively. She needed advice, for it had been three days since she had spoken to Mr. Farnsborough. Three days she held a secret that would free Sir Roland from Letty's grasp. Three days and she was no closer to her objective...but Lady Bussingham would not approve. She would say that Sir Roland must be told immediately about his inheritance. She would say too that now it was time to end her deception and she just couldn't do that!

"'Tis Letty's ball tonight...I just can't seem to get into a festive mood...I don't know, Aunt Jana...this ball of hers, it portends trouble," she said at last sharing something of her fears.

"How so, my love?" Jana Bussingham was no fool. She had not missed the fact that Lacey Burton was fast falling in love with Sir Roland.

"'Tis Sir Roland...he means to have Letty and she is all wrong for him. She won't make him happy, Aunt Jana...she won't..."

"No, probably not, but that is not why marriages of convenience are contracted, my dear. You are old enough to understand my meaning, so we need not go into that any further."

"But...but..."

"But what? You are in love with Sir Roland and want him for yourself, is that the problem you are facing?"

She couldn't speak so she nodded and then moved again in a desperate fashion. "You don't understand..."

"I do, Lace, I understand completely. You will lose him. He is not the boy to throw away practicality on an ideal."

"I don't agree. I think there is that in him that will give in finally. I think he will yield...I think he will choose me in the end. Aunt Jana . . . he loves me . . . I just know that."

Lady Bussingham shook her head sadly. The chit was in for a bad case of heartache. Sir Roland was not immune to Lace, that was certainly a fact she had observed, but Sir Roland was a hardened rake with an objective of his own in sight; he would not give in to emotion. However, they were not given the opportunity to continue their argument as the door opened to admit Sir Roland.

Lace broke off to smile up and across at him. He looked a wonder with his auburn waves framing his handsome face. She loved the winged silver hair at his temples, and she allowed her gaze to linger naughtily upon his lips. He sucked in his breath as he met her impish glance and returned her one of disapproval. It was always thus lately. She would flirt with him, outrageously so, and he would attempt to turn her up cold. Not always an easy thing, for he longed to take her up in his arms. He longed to touch her lips with his own and even now he wanted only to cross the room and hold her. He vacillated between relief and irritation at Lady Bussingham's presence, however it enabled him to summon up the required control.

"Ladies," he bent low over Jana Bussingham's outstretched hand, turned and bowed politely at Lace, "I trust you have been amusing yourselves?" It was quietly said, and Lacey could not hide the look of melancholy that suddenly came over her. She couldn't bear it, she thought desperately. How could she sustain his continued seasoning of winter, the frost that shielded him from her? He saw it and his heart moved within. Without even realizing it, his legs were commanded and he found himself standing far too near to her.

He couldn't speak because he wanted to comfort her and had no right to do so. She looked up and found his eyes and understood. Lady Bussingham took leadership over the proceedings and said lightly, "Amusing ourselves? Nonsense! We have been bored to tears. It is dreadfully tiring to have to rest oneself in preparation for a ball!"

He chuckled. "Ah, but think of the rewards!"

"Those rewards, my dear, are for the young, like yourself and our lovely Lace." She sighed. "My sensibilities forbid my dwelling on what is left to we poor dowagers!"

He laughed. "Doing it up brown, ain't you, my lady? I'd wager a monkey you won't be left to the dowager's tongues but will be out on the floor waltzing every dance!"

The door opened once again to exhibit a flustered kitchen maid. She dropped a leg and begged pardon, explaining quickly and not too coherently that there was some problem requiring m'lady's arbitration below stairs. Lady Bussingham sighed, excused herself and left Lacey and Sir Roland alone.

Sir Roland's brows drew together and he moved away taking up a corner position. Lace observed this and her sense of humor tickled her. "Afraid, sir?"

He stared at her. "*For you*, minx, yes."

She stalked him slowly, irregularly, walking as though toward a circle and ending very near his chin. She looked up. "Why, for me?"

He gave a short laugh and pinched her cheek which he immediately regretted, for the touch was like static going through his fingertips and giving him cause for relief. He wanted to take her in his arms and somehow his hands found the curve of her shoulders.

"Lace, Lace...don't you see what I am...don't you understand?"

"What do you think?"

"I think you have made me a hero and cannot see the forest for the trees!" he said on a bitter note.

"And you see yourself the villain?"

"Something like that..."

This time she gave off a short laugh. "But, sir ... so do I."

He straightened. "But, Lace..." She had caught him off guard.

"Oh...am I wrong? Then I give you leave ...defend yourself."

He let go of her shoulders and turned his back toward her and was again disconcerted as she ducked beneath his arm and was once again facing him. He scowled at her. "No, you are not wrong, and I shan't defend myself."

"Very well, then. We are agreed that you are a villain. Take me, then. Do you not want me? Yes, I can see that you do...so why do you stop? Love me here and now, sir, and forget about tomorrow."

He stepped back in utter shock, for he had missed the twinkle in her eye. "Lace...think what you are saying!"

She was caught up in the spontaneity of this new line of bantering, "Should you not bed me, sir ...perhaps not this moment, not in this room, but sometime soon. 'Tis part of the scheme of things. Villains are forever bedding one lady and marrying another...that is if they marry at all..."

He took her shoulders in a hard grip. "Stop it, Lace!"

She turned deadly grim and her eyes were dark, bright and full with the seriousness of her meaning.

"Then, sir, never call yourself villain to me again!" She pulled herself out of his grip and walked away, making for the door.

He moved to go after her. "Lace...Lace..."

She didn't respond. She didn't look back, though every fiber of her being wanted to turn and run into his arms. Let it go for now, she told herself, get out of here, make him think. She forced herself to walk out of the room and leave him to his decisions.

He watched her retreat and found himself in abject misery. There was nothing to decide; fate had already done that for him. Tonight he would go through with his intentions and ask Letty Rainbird to be his wife!

John Rainbird prided himself on his accomplishments. His father had begun, with an indifferent competence, a small textile mill. Shrewd business sense coupled with ambition and hard work saw them into better days. His father had sent John to Oxford but although his money had bought him his admittance, John had found himself sadly out socially. It had stuck in his belly and when in later years he married and found himself a father, he also found himself determined to enter another world. He would see his daughter married into the quality! Now, in his richly established rooms, he watched the local gentry milling about and was well satisfied. There was Lady Stanhope herself chatting easily with his own wife, and there...Lord Collymore prancing after some pretty dark-haired wench...and his daughter reeling on the arm of Sir Roland. Ah, a noble family there. No duke...but certainly a step up. He patted his round paunch with satisfaction and moved off to greet an arriving crony.

Lacey looked up as a tray of sweetmeats was

offered and was startled to find a familiar face. Her hand went to Lord Collymore's arm as she stopped the servant. "Just a moment...are you not Stills...Lady Stanhope's man?"

"Yes, mum..." said the man nervously.

"Whatever are you doing here...?" she asked in some surprise.

"Oh, its all right, Lace. Mrs. Rainbird was shorthanded...my aunt offered to send over a couple of our people. I think we have a cook somewhere about as well."

Stills took this to mean he was excused and bowed himself away. Lace accepted the explanation but watched the man until a new arrival caught her interest. "Why...there is Charles Teggs! I had no idea he would be here tonight. Come on, Colly, let us go say hallo..."

His lordship was not pleased. Lacey was looking ravishing in her close-fitting silk gown of soft pink. He wanted no competition in his way and a quick glance at the gentleman she referred to made him uneasy. Charles Teggs was far too attractive to be taken lightly.

The viscount appeared at that moment. "Come dance with me, Lace..."

"Not now, Buzzy...Charles Teggs has arrived. I think we should make him feel welcome."

"Don't see that," returned the viscount moodily. "He isn't our guest. We're not hosting this squeeze."

Lace looked about, for when she last had left the viscount, Flora had been beside him. "Where is Flora?"

"Lady Stanhope took her away for some bit of nonsense...but Lace...Lace..." he groaned, for she was already bouncing off to greet the newcomer.

Collymore hastened to follow in her wake, and finding it was better to join her than fight her, the viscount took up the train.

"Mr. Teggs. How good to see you here," said Lace, stopping before him and allowing him to take her gloved hand to his lips.

Mr. Teggs smiled as he brought his face up but finding Lace flanked by two zealous gentlemen he cooled himself and the comment he would have liked to make. "You are as ever, enchanting, Miss Eden."

"Do you hear, Buzzy! He says I am enchanting. You said my dress was cut too low. You said my..."

"Never mind what I said," returned Buzzy irritably, "and dance with me... 'tis a waltz."

"And a lovely one. I shall dance it with Mr. Teggs!" returned the lady.

"But, Lace... *I* said you were ravishing!" objected Collymore. "Surely ravishing ranks higher than enchanting."

"No, enchanting has it." She twinkled and left on Mr. Teggs's arm.

Sir Roland's twirling of Letty brought his glance 'round the dance floor and found Lace in Charles Teggs's arms. His teeth gritted together, and his circling brought him very near her.

"Mr. Teggs," he said merrily enough, "is your balloon all tucked away for the night?"

"Thankfully, yes," returned Mr. Teggs, gazing for a moment at Letty. "Miss Rainbird... thank you..."

"For what...?" she called as Sir Roland spun her prettily.

"Perhaps Mr. Teggs would like to tell you without shouting across the floor?" suggested Sir Roland lightly. He stood to one side, clearly offering up his partner and Mr. Teggs bowed and did the same.

Sir Roland's hand found Lacey's waist and he steered her gently, firmly away as they moved to the cadence of the music. "Neat, my dear sir, very neatly done," complimented the lady. "But you really should not be giving over your future bride to rakehells..."

"Aha! Then you admit our Mr. Teggs is a libertine?"

"I admit it."

"And did you think I would leave *you* to him, minx?"

"But you would leave your intended to him?" she asked incredulously.

"What Letty does in that regard little concerns me," he said coldly.

"But...that is...dreadful..."

"Of course it is, but it is also life."

"So is starving and pain...but we do not look to it. You are walking into a situation...that is...that is..."

"Necessary. Don't, Lace. Don't berate me. Not now when all I want to do is drown in your eyes, in the scent of you...just dance with me...be near me."

"Oh, Roland...Roland...that is all I want, to be near you, but you are making it impossible."

He could see the garden doors. He waltzed her in circles to their edge, stopped and took her hand, passing through into the torchlit night air. She made no objection as he led her away from the house, down a pebbled path to a row of evergreens. A stone bench came into view and he stopped and pulled her to its seat with him and face her. "Lace,...there will never be any future for us. Whatever we feel for each other at this moment...will be forgotten."

"Will it?"

"Damnation, girl, I hope so!"

"Why...don't you want to love me? Would loving me be so very bad for you?"

"Yes, yes, yes! Loving you would be *death* to me! Lace...do you think I could take you for a mistress...*you*?"

"Oh, I see. I was not born low enough. Well, then, I have the solution. All I have to do is get married to that old groat in London...and that should make it all right for me to become your mistress!"

He couldn't answer such a thing. It filled him with rage and he could no longer think. Feelings overrode all else, smashing his good sense and he took her in his embrace. His mouth sought hers and she gave her lips willingly, tenderly, responding ardently as he pressed her closer still. They gave to one another, drawing strength from their passion, from the wonder of their love. She thrilled to him, came alive for him and then suddenly he was pushing her away. She spoke softly, attempting to keep him with her still, attempting to win this small battle, "Don't you see, Roland...this proves you cannot marry Letty!"

"No!" he spat and jumped to his feet. "It only proves me a cad!" He turned and nearly ran in his anxiety to get away from her, from the power she had over him. He had to escape it. He had to leave her unscarred. He had to save her...save himself. What would happen to them if he were to marry her? They would be penniless. What would happen to their love, then? There was only one answer. He rushed into the ballroom and sought out Letty. She stood among her friends, chatting nonsensically. He came upon her and bent over her ear.

"Letty...come with me...now...I cannot wait another moment. Where can we talk...be alone?"

She excused herself from the girls at her side and threw over her shoulder a smug smile to Charles Teggs, who stood watching her from not far away. "We can talk in Mama's tearoom upstairs," she said, leading Sir Roland off.

Lacey sat for a long moment. Sir Roland's departure had left her with little hope. She had throught once he kissed her... the magic of it would win him over. She believed that once he admitted his feeling for her to himself... to her... he would not pursue in his course to marry Letty. A sigh escaped her lips and she got slowly to her feet. Her mind cogitated furiously in variance to the dragging of her feet as she meandered through the lanes of neatly laid-out gardens. There was no way out now. She would have to tell him. She would have to tell him tonight about his inheritance. It filled her with sadness to see the first of her ideals go bleating to its death. Well, there was some small comfort in knowing that he was not in love with her financial standing, that if he were to ask her to be his wife after he discovered that he had inherited, it would at least be for love? If only he had been able to give up all this plaguey business.

Sad, very sad to discover that life, love and happiness were widely different from her childhood fancies. She picked up her spirits, chalked up the experience and started for the ballroom doors. She would have to get to Sir Roland and tell him right away about his inheritance. She arrived at the doorway to find John Rainbird stopping the musicians. Sir Roland stood nervously to one side of Mr. Rainbird, Letty, bright-eyed and excited, stood to his other side. There was something about the scene that made Lace's heart skip a beat. No . . . oh, no . . . Lace started forward but it was already too late. John Rainbird was already happily announcing the *betrothal of his daughter to Sir Roland Keyes!*

Chapter Thirteen

AIR! SHE NEEDED air. Lacey's lungs had ceased their function, her heart seemed to explode within her chest and her eyes could not focus. Over! It was all over ... she had to escape this room. She had to find shelter from his eyes ... staring into hers. Without knowing how, she found herself in the main hallway. She took its length, leaned against the wainscoting for support and reeled into an empty room.

It was dimly lit and unoccupied and she sank thankfully into a large wing chair to collect her thoughts. What could she do? There was no way a gentleman of honor could retract a proposal of marriage. After all, he could not very well say, "So sorry, Miss Rainbird, now that I am a man of means I no longer need to wed you."

"Dear God!" she breathed to the empty room, "He will never forgive me. It is all my fault. He will be tied to that dreadful girl...because of me..."

"What's that you say?" said a familiar male voice from the doorway.

Lace sucked in air as she looked up to find Buzzy coming her way, closing the door at his back. "I saw you rush out of the ballroom, Lace, and thought you might be ill...would have sent Mother...but didn't want to draw a fuss...Lace...are you feeling quite the thing?"

"Oh, no, Buzz...no..."

He went to her immediately and went down upon one knee, his hand sought hers and put it to his lips. "Lace...what is it?"

She patted his head and he sighed, for she had neatly explained by the action just how she thought and felt about him. "'Tis a terrible fix I have got Sir Roland into."

Again the door opened and another familiar male voice lit upon her ears. Sir Roland discovered an interesting scene, such as it was, with the viscount upon his knee, Lace's hand tightly held. Something exploded in Sir Roland's stomach, and his voice was hard and dry when it came. "I beg your pardon, Miss Eden. I saw you leave the ballroom...and was concerned. However, I see you are in excellent hands..." He hesitated, but as neither Lace nor the viscount tried to recall him he left the room.

The viscount rose and there was a frown in his blue eyes. "Lace, perhaps I shouldn't mention this...but I think Ro there...has a *tendre* for you..."

"What a very odd thing to say to me when he has just asked Letty to be his wife!" she snapped, and then immediately retracted, "Oh...please forgive me, Buzzy...I am quite distracted."

"Yes, I should think you would be!" returned the viscount caustically. "I mean, if you had only been truthful with Ro...he would have asked you to be his wife and not that shrew..."

She was startled. "Truthful? What do you mean?"

"What do I mean? Exactly what should I mean? If you had told Ro your real name..."

"Oh, Buzz! Then he would be marrying *me* for my money..."

"Not so! There is no harm in loving a rich girl..."

"But I would never have known...at any rate, that is not the problem."

"What is?"

"Oh, Buzz...I can't tell you...but I must find a way of telling *him*...and Buzz...when I do...he will never forgive me!"

She moved toward the hall door, opened it and waited only for Buzz to join her. As they turned down the corridor she saw Flora coming out of the library. She called to her but such was Flora's flustered state that the girl did not hear her. Lacey frowned as she watched the girl limp hurriedly up the stairs to the next floor. She turned to find Buzz totally absorbed in Flora's movements, and she smiled naughtily. "She *is* lovely, isn't she?"

"Quite, quite lovely..." His silly grin, however, turned into a frown as the library doors opened once again to disclose Lord Collymore. He saw Lace and the viscount and came languidly toward them. So, thought Lace, that was the reason for Flora's distress? Collymore had been plaguing the poor girl with his advances! Evidently the viscount was of the same opinion and gave Colly a heavy set down by raising his quizzing glass.

Collymore laughed goodnaturedly. "I have one...gold rimmed, you know. Should I do the same?

137

He added reproachfully, "No, I think not, we both need not make cakes of ourselves."

"Colly, I think you are horrid!" snapped Lace, stomping off. He sighed. The girl was too quick-witted. She had already deduced that he had been dallying with the little lame Flora. Very well, perhaps he would have to give up that sort of thing for a while. He didn't want Lace jealous, for a jealous female was the devil to deal with! He followed her, his face a mask of apology.

The viscount reached out and held Collymore back a moment. "Doug...hold a minute, I want a word with you."

"Do you? I can't imagine why," said Collymore dryly. He pulled out of the viscount's grip.

"Can't you? But then, you were never very needle-witted..."

Collymore wagged an admonishing finger. "Careful, friend...careful!"

"Precisely my advice to you. I don't want Lace hurt."

"Nor do I, Buzz...nor do I."

"Then leave her be, Doug. She ain't up to snuff...she ain't up to you."

"You are doing it rather too brown, ain't you? You want the chit for yourself. All right, then, you have my leave to have a go at her. The chit won't have you. She wants excitement and you are not the sort to give it to her."

The viscount felt very much like planting Collymore a settler. Good sense and some control kept his itching fist at his side. Truth? Was there any truth to what Collymore was saying? Did he want Lace for himself? Was he too dull for her?

Collymore didn't wait for more but laughed and

stalked off toward the ballroom. A heavy sigh escaped the viscount, and he too left the hall.

Inside the library a lone figure moved from behind the long, brown velvet drapes. Damn, but he had nearly been nabbed that time! That lame girl had come in upon him and he had just managed to dive out of sight. Good thing flash 'imself came in. Well, they was gone now and he best be getting on with it! Quickly, quietly he slid the long window open and lowered a large, worn leather pouch onto the earth below!

"Coo now...curst business...me taking all the risks...him lording it in the ballroom!" He moved away, sighing over the remaining treasures in the cabinet he had just poached. But, guv' now...he said to take nought but those gold loving cups. Said as they could be melted down...and guv' now...he was a knowy one. Gingerly he opened the door a crack and listened. No one lingering about. Good. He opened the door wider and peered out. Safe. Unseen and unhampered he departed and went about his business, for there was no one about to suspect and stop him.

In the ballroom much excitement followed the news of Letty's engagement to Sir Roland. People milled about the couple offering felicitations, advice, encouragement and various opinions on the state of matrimony. Lace entered the scene and avoided Sir Roland's face as she moved to find Lady Bussingham.

"Aunt Jana..." she called as she gently pulled the woman's arm, "I have to speak with you."

"Now, love?" She scanned Lace's face. Of course it

139

was the announcement of Sir Roland's betrothal that had upset her. "Of course...come, we'll take a little walk, shall we...?"

However, they were given no opportunity to do so for Mr. Rainbird again called for everyone's attention. "A toast, my friends! We must drink a toast!" With which he turned, spotted Stills and called the lackey to order. "Come here, man...take this key"— he handed it over—"and go to the library cabinet and bring the gold loving cups!"

Stills bowed and left to do his bidding, while at his back glasses of champagne were being put into the guest's hands! Charles Teggs had found a corner from which he quietly watched the proceedings. So, then, the heiress was lost to him? Letty looked up from the crowd that surrounded her and scanned the room, stopping as her eyes found his face. He smiled and tipped his hand to his forehead. She flushed and turned away, and he smiled to himself. She was not indifferent to him...? He then discovered Lace's agitated face. Beautiful, even now with something troubling her, and he could see that something certainly was. She was no heiress...but maybe a pleasant enough pasttime? He inched his way toward her and touched her elbow, bringing her face 'round to his own.

"Oh...Mr. Teggs...have you been enjoying the ball?"

"No, not really."

"Nor I!" she said forgetting to guard her tongue.

"Perhaps we could console one another?"

"Console? Do you need consolation?"

"Very much, and I cannot think of anyone better suited to bring me out of my doldrums," he said, his eyes flirting with her.

She smiled impishly. "Oh...I don't know, I

can ... but she is now spoken for. Is that the reason for your blues?"

"You are, my dear"—he touched her nose—"far too intuitive for my comfort."

She sighed, "What we both need at this particular moment is an understanding friend and a strong shoulder."

He glanced sharply from her to Sir Roland and nodded in quick comprehension. "I see ... well, then, take a stroll with me, for I doubt that either of us wishes to be present for the toasting."

She hesitated and looked toward Jana Bussingham, who was in deep conversation with a friend. If she didn't talk to someone she would surely burst, but was Charles Teggs the right one to confide in? No, she didn't think so. Instinct cautioned her but fate spared her making an excuse, for Stills had returned with the excited report that the cabinet had been broken into and the loving cups stolen from their resting place.

"What?" shrieked Mr. Rainbird. "That is impossible ... those cups are valuable antiques ... you must have gone to the wrong casing ..."

"No, sir, oi tell ye the lock 'as been tricked open ... and the cups be nabbed!" returned the lackey nervously.

Silence enveloped the room. No one spoke for what seemed an interminable time. However, the quiet was soon broken by Mrs. Rainbird who felt it appropriate to the occasion to let go a scream and sink into her future son-in-law's arms.

Sir Roland suddenly seemed to be omnipresent as he laid Mrs. Rainbird down, ordered a servant to bring in smelling salts and requested the company at large to be calm and collected. He then asked that no one leave the room but chose to do so himself, leaving

Mr. Rainbird to groan and carry on behind him.

In the hall, Sir Roland requested a lackey to fetch the local magistrate before he went to the library to inspect for himself the truth of the servant's report. He examined the cabinet and discovered that the lock had indeed been forced open but in such a way as to make him fairly certain that the thief had been a man of experience. He glanced 'round the room quickly for some other signs of disturbance but finding nothing he soon returned to the ballroom and found something of a commotion.

Women were in hysterics, exclaiming that there were cutthroats lurking about and begging their gentlemen to see them safely home. Their gentlemen seemed inclined to arm themselves and go in search of nefarious criminals, and everyone seemed to be talking at the same time.

Sir Roland managed to get their attention by smashing a nearby champagne bottle. Mrs. Rainbird had come out of her faint only a moment ago and the sound of crashing glass sent her back into the realms of semiconsciousness; however, the explosive sound did catch the required attention.

"I suggest that the best thing under the circumstances would be for all of you to return to your homes. I have sent for a magistrate who will know best what next should be done. Please calm your ladies and yourselves...and go home!"

As no one had anything better to offer or to argue, the company at large began complying with this suggestion. Only Lady Stanhope wished to stay, but Collymore insisted on taking Flora and his aunt home.

Lace lingered as the viscount and his mother took their leave of the Rainbirds and she turned to Sir Roland. "Of course... *you* are staying?"

His glance was frigid. It was as though he had never kissed her in the garden, as though he had never felt anything for her at all...worse, it was though whatever he had felt had turned into dislike. "Could you doubt it?"

She picked up her skirts and hurried after Lady Bussingham, but the viscount stopped them at the door. "Mother...do you think I could put you in the coach with Lace and send you off home? I really think I should remain behind with Ro...he shouldn't have to handle this alone."

"I think, dear, that is an excellent notion...I feel certain Roland needs a friend at the moment," returned his mother as she took up Lace's arm and led her to their waiting coach.

Chapter Fourteen

A NIGHT TO rival many. Such was the size and glitter of the stars, such was the brightness of the moon, still and quiet the trees, yet a lone rider had reason to curse its gleaming loveliness. He jumped nimbly off his horse and tethered it securely to a birch. There he stood a moment, his cloak tightly wrapped 'round his broad shoulders. His hat was pulled lower over his forehead, for he had good cause to keep his features averted from detection. Slowly, steadily and cautiously he made his way through the woods, picking his way carefully toward the gardens that flanked the Rainbird house. There he paused another moment to take in his surroundings and ascertain his next direction. From where he was, he could just pick out the library windows and it was to one of these in particular that he chose a path.

There, at last! His hand reached out and closed on a worn, leather satchel, and he smiled to find it heavy with its prize. Quickly he raced across the lawns and stopped to look back in time to see the magistrate arriving at the Rainbird's front doors! This brought a smile to his mouth. He loved the excitement it instilled in him as much as he loved the money such dealings brought. Right under their noses! He had dished them all!

He reached his horse, paused a moment to peer into the leather pouch at the gold cups within. These he would sell in the morning, for he needed ready cash. Most of the gems they had stolen at the London routs were not yet safe enough to liquidate, but these gold goblets were a different story. He laughed softly and mounted his animal. It had been an easy enough job tonight. He had been worried for a long moment when John Rainbird had sent Stills after the cups. That was something he had no way of anticipating beforehand. No, he had thought the theft would not be detected till morning and with any luck, perhaps not until days later. But, no matter, it really did not signify for there was no possible way they could trace it to him. His man had done a neat job and now what was left was to make it pay!

Sir Roland and the viscount had moved into the library. Mr. Rainbird had left them alone while he saw to his lady above stairs. Letty had been asked to go to her room, which she did quite happily as she had begun to feel bored with all the fuss over the missing goblets.

"Well, Ro...you have done it, haven't you?" said the viscount on a sigh. It was the first moment they had alone together since the announcement of Sir

Roland's engagement to Letty and the question hung heavy on the air.

Propriety forbade Sir Roland from answering honestly, friendship demanded it. He smiled ruefully. "So I have...but remember old boy...I had no options."

"Damn! You will regret it all the rest of your days, Ro...damn, but I wish you had an out."

"Buzz...regret it all the rest of my days? Don't you see...? No, I can understand that my predicament is beyond your understanding..."

"I resent that, Ro! I understand fully...it's just that I—I rather thought you might find another way?"

"Another way? Look here, Buzz...you know why I came to Bussingham in the first place! I came to escape my creditors and to marry the heiress Rainbird! Harsh as it sounds...it is! I make no excuses for myself...or for her. We have made our choice and love had nothing to do with it...for either of us. Take comfort in that!"

"Take comfort in that?" ejaculated the viscount. "Are you daft, man? Do you think I am questioning you for fear that you might be hurting Letty? Damn it, man, I know what she is...what she will be in time...Do you take me for a fool?"

"Then why do you prod me, Buzz? Don't you realize what this decision has cost me?"

"I...I thought in the end you might find another means to your end..."

"Did you, by God!" It was an outraged sound born of pain. "What, then...am I all powerful that I could stave off Debtor's Prison forever? Did you think I would take my name...the name of Keyes through the mud? No, my friend..."

The viscount stopped his frenzied movements and stared long at his friend. "No...I didn't really think...I imagined...another way could be found..."

"You have never been in such a fix. Money has always surrounded you. Your finances have always matched your name...your position."

The door opened and the butler announced a Mr. Jacot. The man who followed the name was somewhat small, round and encased in clothes both disheveled and sorely in need of repair. However, he had a pair of keen, dark eyes that Sir Roland was quick to discover.

"I'be been tolld thare be a woonder of happenings 'ere, sech as staling and its like," said Mr. Jacot in a strong Yorkshire dialect to no one in particular. He moved into the room and began examining the cabinet in question.

Sir Roland leaned back and his eyes began to twinkle, but the viscount found Mr. Jacot's behavior objectionable. "Just a moment, sir, I think you had better wait for Mr. Rainbird..."

"Do ye think so indeed? Wisht wit ye now. 'Tis mucky pride forever interfering wit me and me wark, but raight then, who might ye be...spake, I give ye leave."

The viscount was somewhat taken aback but he managed to answer that he was the Viscount Bussingham and that the gentleman beside him was Sir Roland Keyes.

"Raight then, what 'ave ye to do wit all of this?"

"Well...nothing...we were guests here when the cups were discovered missing."

"How do ye happen to be still here whilst nobbut yerselves stayed on...?"

"Perhaps I may answer that," put in Sir Roland

politely but firmly taking over. "I am engaged to marry Miss Rainbird. The viscount is an old friend and we stayed on to help the family."

"Raight ye are!" said Mr. Jacot, for this confirmed the butler's tale which he heard before he had entered the library. "Now, then ..." He moved directly to first one window and then the next. It was at the second window that he made a sound, that being, "Wisht now ..."

"What is it?" asked Sir Roland, standing erect with some interest.

"This window, sir...'tis unlocked whilst the other...it ain't, if ye get me drift..." He began to open the window. This done, he took up a stick of candles and hanging over the low window's ledge began clucking with his tongue. "Good soft earth ..." He straightened, bumped his head on the rim of the open window, rubbed it and said, "I'll be back directly..." and was gone.

Sir Roland and the viscount exchanged glances before both fell to laughing. It was thus that Mr. Rainbird found them and said in shocked accents that he did not think either of them had any sensibility, laughing at a time like this.

Sir Roland wiped his eyes and apologized saying that it was just a release of tension. This seemed to appease Mr. Rainbird, and they were soon revisited by Mr. Jacot.

"What did you find, Jacot?" asked the viscount.

"Thares been dealings this neeght. So then, I 'ave a few questions that'll need answering."

"Like what? I don't see how we are going to answer anything...none of us knows anything," whined Mr. Rainbird. "Those cups were worth a fortune...you will certainly be able to trace their whereabouts...?"

"Not all the warld could trace 'em down. Our culls

now...they be prime culls...up to every rig. They'll be melting those goblets down, they will," answered the magistrate. "So then...can ye be telling me who might have come in and out of this room tonight?"

"No one!" answered Mr. Rainbird. "I gave strict orders to all the servants...they were not to go in here...and I'm sure none of the guests would have wandered in here..."

"Well as to that, almost anyone could have come in here," returned the viscount.

"Have you someone in mind?" asked Sir Roland sharply.

"Miss Morely...Lord Collymore...they were both in here...they may have seen a servant wander in or out..."

Mr. Jacot took quick notes with his quill before eyeing the viscount inquisitively. "Whet, then...how did ye happen to see this Miss Morely and Lord Collymore?"

"I was...in the hall at the time," he said lamely.

"Was there anyone who could confirm this?"

"Why should anyone have to?" snapped the viscount.

"Och then, mucky pride again. It would help, m'lord...?"

"I have already told you who I saw coming out of the room. You may take it for what it is worth," returned the viscount bitingly.

Sir Roland eyed him for a long moment as he knew very well that Lace had been in his company, and then he steered Mr. Jacot into new areas.

"Plain as pikestaff! You are in the basket, Lacey Burton," said Lacey to herself as she plumped sadly onto her bed. Peewee jumped up and curled himself 'round her feet. "Oh, dog...dog of mine...he is going

150

to marry Letty...'tis all my fault. He will hate me when I tell him...I must find a solution before they set a date, I just must!"

A knock sounded at her door and she called out to find Lady Bussingham on the other side. "Come in, Aunt Jana..."

The door opened and her ladyship, now dressed in a mauve silk wrapper over her night dress, popped her head into the room. "Darling...I know you wanted to talk to me earlier and then with all the excitement...we never did get the chance. I thought you might still..."

"Oh, yes Aunt Jana..." said Lace, sitting up and patting a spot on her bed. "I've really done it this time, I mean...not only to myself...but to Sir Roland as well."

"I know, dear...I understand, but you will get over him..."

"No. You don't understand. It's more than just the lie about who I am. Oh, Aunt Jana...you will think me a dreadful girl and indeed I am, I am..."

"I could never think that, so tell me what scrape you have strayed into and we shall make it right between us."

When Lacey had at last finished her woebegone tale, she had to sniff to hold back her tears. She could see by Jana Bussingham's shocked expression that this time it was more than a scrape she had plunged headlong into. This time it would take a great deal of doing to set things to rights.

"Now, now, Lace, maudlin tears won't help, and I shan't scold, for what's done is done. You have managed to take your fence flying and land yourself in the ditch! 'Tis time now to stand and check for damages."

"I've done that and they may be irreparable."

"Then cut your losses and get on with the business of living! Tell him in the morning, Lace. The longer you wait the more reasons you will find to keep it from him. Tell him."

"No. I can't...not just yet."

"Think, Lace...he may find a solution to this dilemma...he might find a way out of this engagement with Letty...She doesn't love him...he might be able to come up with something while we can't."

"No...if he can think of something...then so can I. Don't you see, Aunt Jana...if I tell him now...he will hate me. I would lose him...but if I told him...and presented him with a solution at the same time..."

"Then find a solution and quickly...for I promise you, Lace, if you don't tell him soon...I will and I shall tell him the whole."

"You cannot mean that, Aunt Jana...he must not hear it from anyone but me..."

"Then let him hear it from you."

"'Tis so hard, Aunt Jana..."

"But necessary!"

She nodded her head miserably for there was no gainsaying that sooner or later, Sir Roland would find out the whole!

Chapter Fifteen

LETTY URGED HER horse forward. He was lazy and she gave him a swift kick, for she was in no mood to brook resistance of any sort. She should be overjoyed but her experience last night proved one thing to her: she would never love Sir Roland Keyes!

To be sure, his kiss, when she accepted to be his wife, had been a dazzling experience that had sent desire coursing through her veins. His touch, when his hand strayed to her waist, had certainly made her press her body closer to his and yet...something, something she could not name, was totally missing!

It was Charles. Always it would be Charles. No other man's voice had the power to turn her blood into bubbling streams. No other man's touch was like his. Even Sir Roland, with his dexterous experience, failed to make her forget Charles Teggs. What could she do? Marriage to Sir Roland would be pleasant enough for he would not make any demands upon her. A lowering thought swept through her that Roland only made love to her because it was the required thing under the circumstances. She had seen no real desire in his eyes. Perhaps that was why she was here, riding the dales to get to Charles Teggs. In Charles's eyes there always flashed fever and she knew he fevered for her. Unfaithful he had been but he wanted her... wanted her more than Sir Roland ever would.

She sighed with relief to see him bending over his balloon basket and she called out his name. He looked up, stashed something quickly into the lining of the basket and moved to meet her. She slid into his waiting hands and without either one uttering a word they found each other's arms and she surrendered to his embrace, to his kiss. At length she sighed, "Charles... this is madness..."

"It is madness that you have promised yourself to another man!" he said harshly, almost bitterly. The thought had occurred to him last night that if ever he would love a woman, be driven by desire for a woman, it would be Letty!

"Charles... what could I do...?"

"You could marry me!"

"Father would never countenance our union. He might even cut me off... then where would we be... you have little enough living, without adding a wife."

"Your father would not cut you off. You are his only child, and I am not anyone to sneer at. My living is such that we would survive for a time without your father's help. Tell him, Letty... tell him you have made a mistake... that you want me..."

154

She moved away, shaking her head sadly; she could not look at him. "'Tis impossible. Think of the scandal if I were to do such a thing now!"

"To perdition with the scandal! Think of all our lives if you do not call it off."

"No. Oh, Charles...it won't be so bad, after all...Roland won't forbid me my pleasures...nor I his..."

"And do you think that would suit me?" he gnashed his teeth and took hold of her shoulders. "Will it suit you to sleep with him and then rush to my arms?"

"Charles!" She was shocked. She hadn't thought about the realities of marriage.

"Well? You cannot answer. Go away, Letty. If you have come here to torture me, you have done the job well...it is unbearable for me to continue in this vein."

She lowered her head. How could she leave him? How could she stay? The entire world had gone insane. "Help me mount, Charles."

He hoisted her into her sidesaddle, and she bent toward him.

"A last kiss, then, my love..."

He took her face almost roughly and his mouth delighted her with his pent-up passion. "No, my Letty...you know very well it is not our last. In the end... *you will be mine!"*

Early morning sunshine did little to assuage Lacey's agitation. She gravitated from one extreme decision to another and ended by chucking them all to the devil and foreswearing thought. Exercise is what you need, she told herself, and made her way to the stables. Refusing assistance, she tacked her horse, discarding the lady's saddle for the flat. She pulled herself into position, neatly laid out her riding skirt around her and moved him out.

Cricket was in high spirits and threw his head quite ready for a run but she held him in check, making him walk down the drive in a sedate fashion until she arrived at the open road. She clicked her tongue and they surged forward into a canter. After a time she reined in and slowed to a trot. He snorted and she laughed at his antics as he pranced with his desire to run. Where to? she asked herself. "I could pay a visit to Flora this morning..." she mused out loud. "And I could see Charles Teggs on the way. Very well, then, Cricket... to the field!"

She discovered the pasture gate closed and took him back some pace. Putting him into a canter she went forward in her seat and took the fence easily, both landing in style on the other side.

She could see Teggs's balloon in the distance and she could see a female rider. Letty Rainbird! Whatever was she doing with Charles Teggs.

Letty espied Lace just about then and pulled her horse up short. What she certainly did not wish at that particular moment was a head-on collision with Lace. Purposely, she turned her horse and took another field. It would be a longer route home but worth avoiding Lace and her inquiring eye.

Lace watched Letty's movements with some surprise. The girl was certainly going out of her way to avoid her. And then a mild suspicion crossed her mind. Letty and Charles Teggs? Things were even worse than she had realized. She no longer felt the desire to ride up to the balloonist and made a wide cut to avoid his point of vision.

Some moments later she was being shown into the morning room of the Stanhope Estate. There she found Flora pouring tea for Lady Stanhope.

"Miss Eden..." said her ladyship, her tone not unwelcoming. "Do come in and join us for tea."

"Thank you." She turned to Flora and gave her a warm smile and was quick to note the nervous twinge to the girl's eyes.

"I trust I find you both in spirits ...?" said Lace, glancing only obligingly at Lady Stanhope and then long at Flora.

"Terrible business, and one does worry when one does not have a man about." She sighed heavily. "However, thank goodness Collymore is with me, for I am persuaded I shouldn't go through with Friday's rout otherwise, you know."

Lace sipped her tea. "Ah, Collymore...he is not here, I presume?"

Flora lowered her eyes. "He mentioned something about having some business to attend to in town."

"So that is where he is off to! I wonder at him not leaving me some word...how is it you know, Flora?" This from Lady Stanhope, and she made no secret of the fact that she was displeased.

"I...happened to be here when he stopped by earlier...you had not yet come down..."

"Oh, I see..." said Lady Stanhope accepting this.

Lace now thought she knew the reason for Flora's agitation. Collymore was up to his tricks. She would have to do something about that...

The door opened and Lord Collymore stepped into the room. He waved a bow to the ladies present, dropped a kiss upon his aunt's cheek and then moved forward to Lace. Sweetly he caught her eye, gently, smoothly and with much adroitness he told her much as he raised her hand to meet his lips and yet not a word did he speak.

"My lord, I see that your trip into town has left you much in spirits," teased Lace.

"Indeed ... for I have come into some of the ready."
He beamed.

"Oh ... how so, Doug?" inquired his aunt curiously.

"A wager, dear ... an excellent wager of mine paid off quite nicely."

Lace rose suddenly. "Well, I had better be getting back."

"Must you go so soon ...?" It was a distressed sound from Flora.

Lace moved to pat her arm. "Don't worry, Flora ... we'll have more time the next time I visit. Perhaps Lady Stanhope will spare you to me one afternoon, for I must do some shopping and should so like someone of my own age to accompany me." She looked pointedly at Lady Stanhope, hoping desperately the woman would offer Flora up willingly.

Lady Stanhope sighed. She was not, after all, a mean-spirited woman. "I think that would be lovely for you both."

"Allow me to walk you to your horse, Lace ..." offered Collymore as Lace started to take her leave.

"Doug ... I am certain Miss Eden would prefer to have her horse brought up from the stables," put in Lady Stanhope a bit too hastily.

"Would she?" said Collymore to Lace, and his eyes twinkled.

She liked him when his face took on such laughter ... it was just too bad he was so unprincipled and shallow. "As a matter of fact, Lady Stanhope, I would rather walk to the stables. It is such a fine day." She wanted a few moments alone with Collymore.

He realized it and his hopes went swooping skyward as he took up her arm. At last. The chit was finally giving over to his charm. Last evening he had begun to have his doubts of ever winning her in the normal fashion, and he had even considered sending for Lace's stepmother.

Once outside, Lace turned her pretty face upward and gave him an arched look that nearly took his breath away. "Colly...I am much distressed..."

"Are you, my love? Only tell me who has bothered you and I shall run him through!" said the gallant.

"Then I should be further distressed, for you are the culprit, Colly." She pouted her lips admirably.

"I? I have upset you? Only tell me how...or shall I cut out my heart and serve it up for your delectation?"

"Stop it, cad! I am being serious," she said, giving his hand a rap, allowing him to catch her fingers, allowing him to put them fervently to his lips.

"You have been deceiving me," she said after a long pause.

"Never! I would have my tongue removed before I would ever do such a thing to you."

"Stop being so confounded bloody!" she said with some show of impatience and then quickly pouted again. "I am speaking of your pointed...attentions toward Miss Morely!"

"Who has put such notions in your head?" he demanded and affected outrage quite nicely.

"You must understand that Flora and I are friends. We confide in one another..."

"Then she has misunderstood my kindness!"

"Perhaps...but Lady Stanhope too is displeased with all the favors you shower upon a hired companion..."

"Lace...Lace...I was only pleasant to the lame little..."

"Stop it!" she cut him off, suddenly very upset. "Don't speak of her in such a manner!" Then remembering her purpose, she caught the further rebukes before they were aired and calmed her voice to a jealous pitch. "If you want me, Colly...really want me...you must prove it to me. You hurt me in the past...feigning an interest in me when it was Daphne all the while."

"No, Lace...you never understood. It was you I wanted...but Daphne stood in our way. I had to appease her..."

This was more than she could stand. "Oh, please, Colly..."

"Only listen to me. I was a fool for a time, Lace, but that is past...it is over."

"Then do not start something new with Miss Morely, for I tell you frankly, Colly, I will not share you." It was coyly said.

"Won't you, my love?" He pulled her up close. "Then do you care for me...you must...say it. I need to hear you say it."

What had she done? She had gone too far. She attempted to pull gently out of his grasp but did not get very far, so she said sweetly, "Colly...you have still to prove yourself before I will commit myself to you. Do you understand me...?"

"I shall endeavor to avoid all female beings in the future. If I see a damsel in distress I shall allow the dragon to eat her!" he said stoically.

She laughed. "Sad is to say...I think you would...but not of love for me."

"Lace..." he objected, his tone most hurt.

They had by now reached the stables and Cricket. Lace pulled at the girth and found it still loose, so she attempted to tighten it, but Collymore took over. She thanked him and positioned herself for a leg up. He hoisted her easily and after situating herself in the saddle, she gave her hand. "Now, remember, Colly..."

"Do but tell me, Lace, my love...how could I forget?"

She smiled to herself and with a click of her tongue she was moving out and down the drive to the main pike. Well, then, she thought reflectively, with any luck, Flora's problems are at an end for I don't think he will allow a moment's indiscretion to ruin his chances at securing my fortune. Now, all I must do is solve my own devious puzzle and somehow free Sir Roland!

"Really, ma'am, we cannot have Lace running about the countryside unattended!" complained the viscount to his mother as he paced to and fro in the library of his home.

Roland frowned and made an impatient gesture with his hand,

"Stop riding grub over your mother, Buzz!" He too was pacing. "Good lord, man, you should hear yourself!" he said with some asperity, far more than was called for. Truth was he too wished Lace would refrain from these solitary jaunts. She had been gone the better part of the morning and had not told anyone where she would be.

"Besides...you cannot immure a girl like Lace," added Jana Bussingham calmly. "She would contrive to escape her shackles and fall into some scrape or other just to prove her independence! No doubt she will bounce her way into this room any moment now."

"That attitude is all very well, my dear...but need I remind you that there is some *rum'un* laying low in the vicinity. I really do think..." started the viscount, only to be interrupted by Lace's entrance.

"Hallo!" called Lace brightly. "Whatever are you all doing gathered in here on such a marvelous morning?" She rather sensed she had landed herself in the suds again and was dearly hoping to stave off a lecture from the viscount.

Sir Roland was acutely aware that the sound of her voice had the power to excite a prodigious sensation in his burning breast. His eyes enveloped her, drew her closer. Forgotten was his engagement to Letty. Forgotten was the vision of Lace in close contact with the viscount last evening and the meaning that vision held for him. Suddenly there was only Lace and his all-consuming need of her. Stop! He heard his mind rant at his heart. What are you doing? He had to get Lace out of his system. He had to force himself to stop feeling.

She wasn't about to let him dismiss her for she could see that was what he was trying to do. His heart called to her, his soul blended with her own and his mind would send her away, if it could, but Lace wasn't about to allow it that power!

Carefully, determinedly she meandered leisurely about the room until she was near enough for him to smell the springtime fragrance of her scent, near enough for him to wish he could reach out and touch her, near enough for him to lose himself in the dark beauty of her eyes.

"Where have you been?" demanded the viscount.

She forced herself to turn 'round and give her attention to the viscount. "For a ride on Cricket."

"To see Charles Teggs, no doubt?" snapped the viscount.

She was aware of Sir Roland beside her and he stiffened as he waited for her reply. She maintained a calm. "I wanted to stop by and see him but changed my mind and went instead to pay Flora Morely a morning call."

"You went *there . . . alone*?" cried the viscount on a

note of disbelief. "How came you to do that, Lace? I credited you with more sense!"

Sir Roland's brows were drawn. "Why shouldn't she go there? You behave as though the Stanhope Estate is plagued."

"It is! With Collymore..." said the viscount, turning once more to Lace. "Look, Lace...don't you think it would be wise in the future to refrain from riding over there alone...I mean...?"

She hastened to stop this line of conversation. She knew well what he was getting at. "Really, Buzz...I don't think Colly would try to abduct me."

"No, indeed!" laughed Roland. "Colly is hanging out for an heiress!"

There followed a disquieting silence, and Sir Roland's penetrating eyes swept the strange expressions of his company. However, Lace broke in hurriedly, "Sir Roland...would you like to walk with me...? I'd like to get some rose cuttings, and you could keep me company."

His voice sounded oddly low pitched, "I would like that...very much, Lace, however I am afraid...I must go out."

"Oh? Riding over to Miss Rainbird's...?" said Jana Bussingham, who was watching both Lace and Sir Roland with growing interest.

"Yes...I think I had better..." said Sir Roland on a note of reluctance.

"To be sure...she will have returned by now," said Lace without thinking.

"Returned? Returned from where?" asked Sir Roland.

She had no wish to make him jealous or to pinch his pride, for that could very well work at cross-purposes with what she wanted, so she hesitated. "From her ride..."

"You met with her this morning?"

"Not exactly...she was crossing through the field..."

"The field. Ah, thus the reason for your avoiding Mr. Teggs," said Sir Roland as though pleased to have a question answered. He had noticed that Letty and Mr. Teggs were more than past acquaintances. It made no difference to him. He was rather amused to see Lace blush. "Is my future bride stealing a march on you with your balloonist, Lace?" He meant only to tease and was rather surprised to see her blush.

Her eyes became pools of fire. He could almost see the flames dart in her fury. "You are odious and unfeeling...and...and yes, you are a rake!" with which she fled the room for the gardens outdoors.

He turned to find Jana Bussingham studying his back and her expression was grave. "That was unwise of you, Roland," she said with a shake of her head. "You are not making any of this very easy for her."

"What, then...shall I be the paragon she thinks me? I cannot," he said on a bitter note that died out before he was able to finish.

"She does not think you a paragon...and perhaps it is too late." She sighed and looked toward the garden doors and then back at Sir Roland.

"I don't understand..." put in the viscount.

Ignoring her son, Jana Bussingham said to Roland, "Go talk to her."

He looked at her for a long moment. "No, it wouldn't be wise. Let her think of me what she will. It will help in the end. Now, if you will excuse me...I had better be going over to pay my future bride a visit."

Jana Bussingham watched him leave and turned

164

to her son, who was strangely quiet. At length he let go a long breath of air.

"By Jove...so the wind lies in that direction, does it? I had no idea!"

"Do you mind, darling?"

He thought about it for a long moment. "Honestly? I don't know...just yet...I really don't know."

Chapter Sixteen

LORD COLLYMORE FINGERED a book without interest and glanced up with some boredom to survey the domestic scene in which he reluctantly found himself. The study was dimly lit by wall sconces and a blazing hearth far too hot for the evening's comfort. Flora sat demurely reading to her ladyship. Flora? She looked a picture with her flaxen hair framing her lovely face. Such a face. A diamond. Too bad about her foot, for otherwise she could have had anyone in all of London...even without a dowry. But never mind Flora. He had to be careful in that regard or he would lose Lace and he had no intentions of losing Lace this time!

Confound Lady Stanhope! She was keeping him on tight rein this visit. He had to breakaway and become independent...totally independent, and he knew the means to that end. He smiled to himself with the thought. The door opened and the candles flickered with the new rush of air. The Stanhope butler stood to one side and announced in a tone that clearly indicated that he thought the intruder beneath his mistress's regard, "Mr. John Jacot."

"What the devil...?" said Collymore, whose eyes had narrowed as he scanned the unusual individual who next appeared.

Mr. Jacot walked quickly into the room and appraised its occupants. He was considered among those who had been fortunate enough to witness his skills, a beadle of the first quality. This, however, was not conspicuously noticeable as Mr. Jacot had about his person an aura of general disarray.

Jacot went directly to Lady Stanhope who sat with her gold-rimmed glass raised to one eye. She did not approve and exhibited this with an uplifted brow and an austere sniff. "Collymore...who is this...creature?"

"Funny now," answered Jacot, "thought I heard that stiff-necked man of yers spake m'name. But then, niver mind, could be ye be that hard of hearing. The name is John Jacot," he said on an amiable note.

Lady Stanhope put up her chin and stared hard across at him. "You sir, are most impertinent."

"Am I? Comes from m'occupation, I suppose."

"And that is?" She was beginning to find herself almost amused by the man.

"Parish Officer and your obedient servant, m'lady," he said respectfully, noting at the same time that both Miss Morely and Lord Collymore seemed more than a little nervous by his presence.

She eyed him with some show of surprise. "Whatever brings you to me, Mr. Jacot?"

"'Twas over m'dinner that it come to me...aye,

thought it best that I make tracks here and speak wit Miss Morely and his lordship before I took me thoughts any further."

"You wish to speak with Miss Morely...and with my nephew...? Why?"

"Wisht now...I don't woonder at yer asking, but 'tis no real fetch, m'lady, and yer not to fret over it. Jest want to verify some information that was given to me last night."

"Last night...oh...then you are here about that dreadful affair at the Rainbird home?" she said, at last understanding some of what he was talking about.

He pulled his head back. "What else would bring me here this time of night, m'lady?"

"What else, indeed? Very well...ask your questions, sir."

He turned to Miss Morely and gave her a long, speculative look. "Aye, then, lass...no need to fret...that's it...jest make yourself easy..." He waited for her to smile and noted that she glanced hastily toward Lord Collymore. "Well, then...it was mentioned to me that ye was in the Rainbird library last evening. Could ye be telling me why ye was there and for what purpose?"

She cleared her throat. She was dreading this. There was Lady Stanhope staring at her, and here she was about to answer this little man's questions and soon it would be out that Collymore had been there with her..."I...I went in to get away from the crush...I thought only to relax a few moments..."

"Aye, then...how long were ye escaping the din?"

"Only a moment or two...then I was joined by Lord...Collymore." She could see Lady Stanhope's expression out of the corner of her eye and it made her cringe within her breast.

"Aye...so I have it. But then, lass...did ye not notice anything strange when ye was in the room...?"

"Strange...? No...I don't think so."

He turned his attention ·to Lord Collymore. "Stalled was ye, lad?" His tone was sympathetic.

"Stalled? I don't understand your question?" returned Collymore cautiously.

Odd, thought Jacot, why were these two so uneasy about being questioned? Very odd. "Bored with the dancing...is what I mean. Ye had to have a reason for leaving all the flowing drinks...food, the pretty ladies...and take on the quiet fashion of a library."

Collymore hesitated, "Oh...yes...that was it."

"Was it? Then ye and Miss Morely were there...ye sat down together and had a nice little chat. Nobbut yerselves?"

"That's right!" said Colly defiantly.

"Mr. Jacot," put in Miss Morely, "I left shortly after his lordship came into the room. It did not appear a seemly situation for us to be...in the library together."

"I should say not!" agreed her ladyship, but she was glaring at Miss Morely not at her nephew.

"Aye, then...ye was left to yer own devices then, lad...did anyone come in upon ye...did ye notice anything out of the ordinary?"

"No one came in and I did not notice anything that seemed strange. I followed Miss Morely out and there encountered in the hall the Viscount Bussingham and Miss...Lace, his house guest."

"Miss Lace...ye mean Miss Eden?"

"That's right."

Mr. Jacot sighed heavily. "Well, then, m'trip out here was much for nought as most of this I already had. But then I thank ye for yer time and bid ye a pleasant evening," he said as he rose to his feet, thinking that both Lord Collymore and Miss Morely bore watching and further investigation.

Lady Stanhope waited only for Mr. Jacot to leave the room before rounding on Miss Morely and her nephew. "So, this has been quite enlightening! I would caution you in the future, Flora, to use more sense. You don't go wandering off into unoccupied rooms...that is asking for trouble"—she turned to Collymore—"as my nephew here has proved. You asked...he answered! Neither of you will engage in such improprieties in the future." Then without allowing either a reply she signaled to Flora, "Now...you may see me upstairs, Flora, and then go off to bed yourself." She turned to Collymore. "And you, sir, have been itching to be off all evening. Very well, then, take yourself off and work out some of your high spirits."

Lord Collymore watched Flora get to her feet and was struck again by the girl's lameness. Really too bad, he thought, and then turned his attention to the future. Confound it all, he had to get out from under!

Letty tore up the note she held to her breast and threw it to the fire blazing in her bedroom hearth. Dare she? He wanted her to meet him in the glen outside her home. Could she? It was nearly nine o'clock...he had written nine o'clock...Oh, yes, she must meet him, if only for the last time! She went to her wardrobe cabinet and pulled out a black cloak. Pulling it 'round her shoulders, she made for the servants stairwell and quietly, gingerly went to the side door. She was out! She stretched the hood of her cloak over her forehead and ran for the thicket bordering her estate. Her parents were out for the evening...she had time...plenty of time. Fleetingly she thought of Sir Roland. No guilt flooded her warm veins. He was thoroughly enjoyable company, but he did not love her. He had stopped by that morning and again for a short time in the evening. Her parents had been present and they had spent a delightful hour in his company. His anecdotes were rich with dry humor...and he was certainly attractive, but at the hour's end it was Charles who came to her mind. It was Charles she wanted with all her heart and soul. After all this time, it was still Charles.

A hand reached out to stop her progress, and she nearly screamed, but she heard his voice, "Darling...oh, my darling...you are really here..."

She turned and found herself in his arms. "I couldn't stay away, Charles. I had to see you again."

He didn't answer this but brought her face up and kissed her long and passionately. When he released her it was to say in a tone meant to indicate his desperation, "Run away with me, Letty...tonight!"

"No. Don't ask me to..."

"You love me...I know you love me. You are no trollop to be here meeting me this way unless it was for love."

"Yes, I do love you...but I owe my parents..."

"You owe *me*...you owe yourself a good life. You can only have that with me."

"Oh, Charles...'tis impossible..."

He answered this by swinging her into an embrace which brought them both to their knees. He could take her, he thought, in a flash. Here and now he could take her virginity and she would feel compelled to marry him. His hand sought her breast but she stopped him. "No...Charles..."

"Letty...Letty...you want me too...you know that you do." His voice was low, hoarse with his desire.

172

"Yes ... but ... oh, Charles ... we cannot," she was pleading.

He let her go with a rush. He was frustrated. He wanted this chit more than he had ever wanted any other. She was hot-blooded, she was ready for him ... yet, he could not force her. The entire thing was growing absurd. Why should he bother? "Go home, Letty!"

"You are angry ... Charles ... don't be angry."

"Go home, Letty ... or I swear I shall have you here and now and then perhaps you will wish me in hell."

"And will you not be in hell if I leave ... ?" There was a teasing quality to her voice. She wanted him to stay here with her. She wanted his arms wrapped around her still. She reached out and touched his hand but it served only to make him jump to his feet.

"Don't torture me, wench! Now ... go home ... if you cannot say you will be my bride, then don't say anything." He waited for an answer and when none came a growl escaped his lips. With a sharp turn of his heel he was gone.

A cry escaped her lips as she watched him vanish into the darkness. "Charles ... oh ..." and she knew herself miserable, more miserable than she had ever imagined possible.

Sir Roland watched Lacey as she picked up her winnings from the card table where she had enjoyed an hour's game with Lady Bussingham and the viscount. He had himself retired with a book but had not read a line. All the hour he could not tear his glance away from her face, from the bubbling movements that were peculiar unto herself. Delightful were all her mannerisms ... how then could he resist her? How ... but he must. He knew he was heading for a heartache ... was already there and there was nought he could do to prevent his world from coming down upon him. His heart had at last received its death march; it would live for no other than Lace.

Resist, he told himself. Don't look at her playful expressions. Don't surrender to her smile. Don't dive full into the depths of her dark eyes...don't...don't! And still he did. Lace...Lace...Lace...his mind rejected and his heart ardently begged. She was all he wanted, all he ever could want and she would never be his.

Lace passed some jest with Lady Bussingham and moved away from the card table. She wanted to be near Sir Roland, needed to be near him. For one wayward moment she nearly plopped into his lap like a naughty child ready for confession. That was how she felt. She wanted to give over the whole truth and make it better, sugar it with affection...but it wouldn't work, not this time, not with Sir Roland. If only she could be alone with him...for just a little while.

As though fate wished to aid in her schemes the Bussingham butler entered the room with a card upon a silver salver and presented it to the viscount. He glanced at it and smiled toward Sir Roland. "By Jupiter...Alfred is in town. He is putting up at the Bull and Horn and begs my company. We are in for a jolly evening...come on then, Ro...let's to horse!"

Sir Roland smiled but there was an apology in it. "No, I think not tonight, Buzz...but do go on, I plan to retire early."

"No...? All right, then. Good night all!" He moved toward Lace and took up her chin. "There now, puss, don't be riding off in the morning without leaving word where you shall be. That is one rule I won't have broken."

"Quite right, my lord." She laughed.

Lady Bussingham went to the door with her son, gave him a kiss and turned to the remaining occupants of the room. "I think I shall call it a night. Don't be too long, Lace." It was gently said. She left them, devoutly hoping Lace would find herself able to tell Sir Roland the truth.

Lace waited for the door to close behind her ladyship. There, she was here with him...alone. She turned toward him and noticed the color in his cheeks, the stiffness to his seat. He looked as though he wanted to escape her. Drat? Why must he be on such guard? "Sir Roland...I suppose the announcement of your engagement to Letty will soon be in the papers?"

"Not until next week...Mrs. Rainbird has only recently lost an aunt...and the month of mourning is not yet ended."

"Good..."

"Good? Don't imagine that a delay of public announcement will change anything..." He got to his feet but she moved to block him from leaving.

"Don't go, Roland...please don't go...not now...I need to..."

He couldn't bear it any longer. Without thinking he took hold of her shoulders. She went willingly into position. So total was her submission that he groaned. All finer principles were sent to perdition as he bent her to his embrace. Only emotion, strong, willful, devastating in its intensity, supreme in its power moved him. He found the sweetness of her lips and communicated his depth of feeling in one searing, enchanted kiss. Even as his mouth discovered her own he would have pulled away, for something went to war within him, but she pressed herself bewitchingly into his body, tempting him still

175

further. They seemed to swirl as his kisses covered her face, her neck and returned to her mouth. She said his name tenderly, lovingly and suddenly he cried as though in agony.

"NO!" He was apart from her and nearly running in his haste to get away.

She reeled and would have called to him but a quiet wisdom kept her silent. She watched him go while his kisses still burned her flesh. Everything was wrong . . . all wrong and it was all her fault. The fault of her pride. She should run after him now and tell him the whole . . . she should . . . but all she could think was that he would hate her. No, she had to find an answer first . . . then she would tell him . . . but where was this answer she sought? Where?

Chapter Seventeen

FLORA MORELY PICKED her way leisurely, thoughtfully over the pebbled drive toward the stables. These days her mind so often strayed to thoughts she had no right to allow herself, yet she couldn't help it. Everywhere she went, everything she did found her overrun with images of one man, the Viscount Bussingham. He was her dream-man come to life. So handsome, so fine, so good, *so unattainable*. How could she...lame ...unendowed...how could she ever hope to catch his interest? She sighed heavily and glanced toward the stables. She so wanted to ride. It was a pleasure she had had to give up when she began working for her livelihood; however, Lady Stanhope had been kind enough to offer up her own mare. The mare was old and sour...but still, it would be a ride.

She felt shy, uncertain about taking up her

ladyship's offer, so she got to the stable doors and hesitated. Perhaps she should think more about it? She began to circle the stable but just as she rounded the corner she stopped short.

"Give over do..." said Stills to the round-eyed, plump woman neatly ensconced in his arms. "There's a pretty mort..."

"Go on, now, ye miserable bruiser!" laughed the woman making no attempt to break away. Stills had come to her ladyship only a few weeks ago but he certainly put some zest into a working girl's life!

"If I thought ye really wanted me off ...why...m'eart would crumble and fall to the wayside. Lord love ye...give Stills one little kiss...there's a fine strapping mort..."

She allowed him his kiss, and Flora went bright red. She had to escape this little scene but as she turned on her heel a loose twig caught and crackled. The guilty couple spun on her and the round-eyed Bess gasped, "So sorry, Miss Morely...I had no idea ye'd be out here looking for me..."

"I...I was not looking for you..." put in Flora hastily, feeling as though she wished she could hide. "Please...excuse me..." with which she turned and rushed into the stables. Well, the decision had been made for her. She would ride. It was the only excuse for her being down here.

Some moments later she was urging her ladyship's mare onto the drive and sedately posting to the aged horse's trot. She was a pleasant enough horse with nice manners and Flora began to relax. She was lonely, desperately so, and just as she reflected dismally on this fact, fate stepped in.

"Flora...Flora...!" It was Lace riding Cricket and coming up quickly from behind.

Flora waved and then used both hands to keep her

horse in check as the oncoming steed excited the elderly mare into motion. As Lacey drew up her horse Flora smiled warmly, "Hallo! Oh, Lace ... you are the very person I need..."

"What is it? What is wrong?"

"Nothing ... and everything ..."

The horses sniffed each other at leisure and discovered there was nothing to fear from each other before their ladies put them into a slow jog. "I don't understand, Flora ... what do you mean?"

Flora's lashes shaded her eyes and there was a blush to her cheeks. "Lace ... I ... I don't want you to think ill of me, for whatever I say might sound very much like a complaint."

"Nonsense. Now tell me ... has that dreadful old woman been harping at you?"

"Oh, no ... my life with her ladyship is not so very bad. You mustn't think she has been unkind to me."

"Nor has she been especially good to you, either," returned Lace sharply. "And Flora ... why shouldn't you complain? If you can't tell your troubles to a friend, then who can you go to? Friends are there to share experiences with ... good and bad."

She smiled ruefully. "That Lace is applicable on both sides. You have troubles of your own ... I can see them in your eyes, yet you never complain about them."

Lace pulled up her horse, "Aha! 'Tis bribing me you are. Done! A tit for a tat! Come on, we'll take up a nice shady spot and exchange sorrows!" She scanned her surroundings, commanded her friend to follow and urged her horse through the thicket to a narrow stream edged with dark-green grass and long-stemmed wild flowers. "Perfect. Dismount, m'girl, and we'll tether up the horses and have a nice long chat."

Flora laughed and hopped off her horse, allowing Lace to take up the reins and see to them. Lace got them settled, found a weathered log, sat with a long sigh and patted a place for Flora to join her. "Now, Flora, m'dear, who shall start? You or I?"

"If *I* started...I really wouldn't know where to begin," sighed Flora.

"All right, then...let me help. I have an excellent notion what is troubling you. *'Tis Buzzy!*"

Flora went scarlet. Was it so obvious! "Oh...why do you say so?"

"Oh, Flora...I am not dim-witted...every time the two of you come within each other's ground I swear I could hear violins!" giggled Lace.

"Then I have been making a fool of myself!" wailed Flora.

Lace patted her hand. "No such thing!"

"You don't understand, Lace. 'Tis not as though I had family to present me...'tis not as though I have a dowry! I have no right to look his way. He...oh...and he would never think to look seriously at me!"

"You are quite wrong...though I do admit he is rather slow about all of this. But he does care for you, Flora...I feel it...see it..."

"If that is true...it only proves my point. He will make no push for me because of my circumstances," she said in a whisper.

Lace frowned. It did appear that the men in her life were mercenary creatures. Even Buzz...for he had no need to marry an heiress, yet it was true, he seemed to almost wish to avoid seeing Flora. Whenever she mentioned riding over to the Stanhope Estate to visit with Flora, he would decline to accompany her. She didn't wish to give Flora false hope.

"I don't know Flora...I used to think that love was all that mattered...but my own situation clearly proves me wrong."

"What do you mean?"

"Now you must promise that what I tell you will be maintained in the strictest of confidence, Flora..."

"Of course, Lace. I would have no right to repeat anything you told me of yourself," said Flora shocked.

"Very well, then...perhaps I should start with a quick summary of how I happen to be at Bussingham in the first place." She took a long breath and began her tale.

A twig in the thicket behind them crackled but neither girl noticed, so involved were they with the meanderings of Lacey's story. Charles Teggs cursed beneath his breath and held his hand over his horse's mouth. He had been out for a ride when he spotted the girls and thought he would stop to chat awhile. As he came upon them he heard Lace speaking.

"So you see...I was so sick of being courted for my fortune that I came up with an alias, but, Flora, it has not served at all!"

Charles Teggs's brow went up. Lace...an heiress? He decided to stay hidden and hear what else the chit had to say.

"But what will you do?" cried Flora. "Lace...you cannot allow him to marry that girl..."

"No, I don't intend that he should...but Flora... how can I stop him?"

"But you must..."

"Flora...you don't know the half of it. You see...not only am I an heiress...but Sir Roland...well, he has recently inherited!"

"But then...why did he...?"

"Because he didn't know it. I sent the barrister

181

away...promising to tell Roland...and then...I didn't tell him."

"Oh, Lace...you have made a muddle of it all."

"Quite!" agreed Lace ruefully.

"But then...what shall you do?"

"Tell him...in the end I must tell him...it is just that I so hoped I might be able to come up with a solution first. He is bound to despise me when he finds out..."

"Oh, Lace...I don't know what to tell you."

Lace patted her hand. "No, I thought not. But there now, you see how much worse things can be?"

Flora broke out into mirth and then gave her friend a warm hug, "You are quite incorrigible, Lace!"

Charles Teggs thought it prudent to make his presence known at this point. Far better to come out in the open than to try and slink away and perhaps be seen. "Good morning, ladies!" he called as he led his horse forward.

The girls looked up and waved, and Lace asked curiously as he approached, "What brings you to this neck of the woods, Mr. Teggs?"

"I was out for a morning ride when I spotted your horses...do you mind?"

"Oh, no, not at all," she answered quickly. "Are you nearly done with the repairs to your balloon?"

"Very nearly. I should be leaving the Nottingham area within the next few days."

Lace stood up. She didn't know why, but she wanted to take Flora and get away from this man. There was something about him this morning that made her nervous. "Well, then, I hope to see you before you go...and I am afraid we must be going now."

He bowed and allowed them to depart without further demure, for he had some thinking he wanted to do alone. However, he did stand looking after them for a long while. "Well, well," he said out loud. "Think of that...the little pretty...an heiress, and right under my nose!"

Lace parted with Flora and made her way home to find the viscount coming through the gardens toward the stables.

"Buzz!" she called and rode her horse up to him. "Will you wait for me? I just want to put Cricket away."

"Of course...but what is it?"

"Nothing, really...I just wanted to talk for a bit."

A few moments later, having left her horse to the groom's care, she came rushing out to take up the viscount's hand and lead him away from the stables. "Now. 'Tis Flora..." she began.

"Flora! What is it...what is the matter with her?" he asked a bit too hastily, a shade too concerned.

She smiled broadly. "*Aha*! So, then, you do care!"

"Care? Of course I care...Lace...what are you about?"

"I want to know...without hedging...without flowery excuses what you mean to do in that direction?"

He turned to face her full and for a moment was completely bereft of speech. When he did at last make a sound it was not a very flattering one. "Brazen little brat! Whatever do you mean asking me such a thing?"

"Don't be so stuffy, Buzz! Answer my question...please."

He frowned, for Flora's image vividly formed before his eyes. "I...plan...to do nought." It was quietly said, all emotion restrained.

"But that is ridiculous! Buzz...*you* are not hanging out for a rich wife...?"

"Flora Morely's family plunged their name into

183

unspeakable scandal. I could not do the same to my own name by uniting it with hers."

Lace stamped her foot. "You are . . . horrid! I cannot believe such words came from your mouth . . . from your mind! How can you? Oh, Buzz . . . you dash all purer beliefs to the ground!" She turned and ran because his words brought tears to her eyes.

Lace was frustrated by realities! Life was turning out all wrong. Fairy tales were never things she thought would come true but neither were demon realms. Everywhere she turned life held out bright, shiny things and they were all marred, terribly marred. Principles she held dear were slashed at every turn and no one defended their honor! People she had believed in were growing twisted and confined . . . and leaving her exposed.

Sir Roland was walking toward her, but such was the state of her agitation that she did not at first see him through her tears. He held her shoulders, firmly detaining her. "Lace . . . what is this?" His finger went to a large salty tear. "Oh, my Lace . . . what has upset you?"

"What . . . oh, no . . . no . . . everything . . . everyone . . . all of you!" She broke free and continued to run. She only knew she had to get to her room, to Peewee . . . had to cuddle him and feel a child again. There was safety in that.

Night came starkly as life stumbled forward, more so in Nottingham's poorer quarters. There, in a dimly lit corner rarely frequented by fellows of taste, stood a worn, dirty and somewhat tilted building whose weathered sign indicated its calling as the "No Place Inn." Its occupants exactly matched the inn's dilapidated condition; however, this evening there was someone who, try as he might to avoid notoriety, stood out among the house's regular patrons.

He was dressed in the fashion of a flash, a gentleman of quality and refinement though his top hat was pulled far too low over his brow and his body form was hard to detect so deeply niched into the corner of the wall where he reclined his chair. Beside him, huddled low over a tankard of ale, was a lesser individual whose garb depicted him as a household servant. He seemed much distressed as he tried to excuse himself to the gentleman in the shadows.

"Lord love ye but I'll swear the mort is ready to cry rope..."

"You have been telling me that now for over a week, Stills!" interjected the flash impatiently. "We took on the Stanhope rig in the first place because you said you would be able to win over her ladyship's maid."

"And so I will. It's jest that this mort has to be 'andled jest so...she is a resty mort full of spirit...I disremember ever having to take it so easy on a wench before but she'll give over...see if she don't!"

"The question is whether or not your courtship will end in her telling you where her ladyship hides the Stanhope Diamonds!"

"She come close on telling me last night, she did...but we was interrupted by some bobbery in the kitchen. Ye got to remember that I don't want this mort getting wise to what I'm about."

"What difference does that make? Damn it, Stills...we'll be long gone before she realizes you had anything to do with it."

Stills shook his head. "Now, guv'...I ain't no green'un to be put off by such a whisker. As soon as they twig the sparklers be missing, 'tis me they'll be looking for," he sighed. "So we'll do it like we planned...or we won't do it at all."

"Damn but there is no time to do it like we planned. The dowager Stanhope's rout is just three nights off... and I plan to be gone that very evening."

"Oh... I don't remember *that* being part of *our* plan..." objected Stills.

"Well, it is now. So, you have to find out where the diamonds are and get to them. How you get away is your own business..."

"Yeah...? And who might be taking the sparklers... *you*?"

"Of course. You don't want to be caught with them..."

Stills shook his head. "Aw, now, guv'... this don't sit with me, no, not a bit."

"Then you will come with me... as we did before... Stills... we've had a good, profitable relationship. I am not about to tip you a doubler..." The gentleman smiled ruefully. "You are far too quick and handy with that sharp-edged chive of yours!"

"Aye, it's good ye remember... me last partner, now he didn't... and all that bounty... it don't do him no good where he is now..." He looked earthward for effect.

"Precisely so." The flash reached into the lining of his greatcoat and when his hand next returned to the round table it was to lay upon it a handful of gold sovereigns. "Those Rainbird goblets fetched a handsome figure... you'll find there more than you expected." He was already getting to his feet, putting an end to the discussion. "I trust you are not displeased."

Stills smiled wide, "Ye ain't deviled me yet, guv', why now would ye start? No, ye've been pound-dealing wit me and I ain't got cause to complain."

"Well, then, Stills, let me hear from you soon for as I said I want to be off before that ball!"

"Aye... I'll be seeing the mort this very

186

night...she'll do." He stood and watched a long moment after the gentleman left the premises. No, he wasn't worried about the guv' tipping him the double. The flash now, he was greedy, but he wasn't stupid. Prudently he pocketed his gold and a few moments later the round table in the back of the No Place Inn housed a different set of men altogether.

It was so easy it made him nervous! Stills slinked across the hall on his way to the dining room. The mort had finally come through this evening and very pleasantly. They had spent a delightful hour in her bedroom and they had laughed over Lady Stanhope's choice of a hiding place for her famous diamonds. In the dining room...in the sideboard beneath a false drawer! It was just too good to be true.

He held the doorknob and pushed open the dining-room door slowly, carefully before closing himself in the room. The drapes were drawn away from the window and there was just enough light for him to work without the aid of candlelight. He stood back a moment from the wallboard cabinet and studied it. He knew his trade well and it wasn't long before he found the spring. He smiled as the door popped and he swung it open, examined and found yet another spring. This opened to exhibit a hidden drawer that was quite empty!

He frowned and studied it but it proved to be too dark for careful examination, so with a reluctant sigh he lit one candle and waved it slowly over the empty drawer. "Ah, then, 'tis a prime place ye 'ave 'ere, yer ladyship!" he said with some excitement, for he discovered that the depth was not quite what it should be. A false bottom was lifted and there sparkling brightly were the entire set of Stanhope Diamonds!

He cooed to himself softly as he lifted them and

dropped them into his shirt. In addition to the magnificent set were a few odd pieces. Thoughtfully, he cupped these in his hand, put the cabinet to rights and speedily left the room. 'Twas a job well done, he told himself proudly. No, the flash, he wouldn't want to be parting wit sech as himself. He was too good at his job.

Chapter Eighteen

LADY STANHOPE SWAYED to and fro before her long, gold-framed looking glass. She was displeased with the image she received. There were too many sags and wrinkles 'round her neck, she had to hide them and the topaz set she chose to wear with the gold silk would never do!

"Bess . . . Bess!" she shouted irritably. "'Tis a good thing I decided to try these things on today . . . for I shan't be wearing them to my rout on Friday! Go downstairs and bring up the Stanhope Diamonds."

"Bring them up, m'lady?"

"Don't dawdle . . . go on . . . they will in all probability need cleaning . . . now go on, I wish to see how they look with this gown!"

The maid dropped a curtsy and mumbling to herself over all the work the dowager set for her to do, she went below, down the hall and into the dining room. There she closed the door behind her, and satisfied that no one was about, she went to work on the sideboard drawer.

Some moments later she was frantically going through all the drawers of the cabinet. It was impossible...and then it dawned on her, the diamonds were gone...really gone!

Stills had seen Bess going into the dining room. He saw the manner in which she closed the door behind her back and he frowned. It was a good thing he had gone out earlier that morning and given over his prize, for if the diamonds were discovered missing, it was more than likely a search of the premises would be made. A search? That gave him a notion, and he fingered the emerald ring he had kept upon his person. There was certainly a method to his cunning he thought proudly to himself as he wound his way upstairs to Flora Morely's quarters. What a prime job he had done! He could still remember the guv's face when he dangled the sparklers before his eyes early this morn. But he'd better hurry now while Flora was in the parlor arranging the flowers. He had to throw suspicion away from himself. There was the dowager's maid...if she were to zero in on what she had told him...if she were to become suspicious, he would need this diversion to get off clean.

The dowager's maid, Bess, sat for quite a long spell trying to remember if there was any other place the diamonds could be, when it finally dawned on her that there was only one answer. This produced a howl of enormous proportions, followed by a series of groans and deafening wails. The butler appeared on the scene, followed closely by the footman.

"The diamonds...they be gone...oh, lordy ...lordy...her ladyship will have m'head...what am I to do...?"

The butler and footman exchanged glances, for indeed this was trouble of no little degree!

The evening had not gone well for Lacey. Sir Roland had gone to dinner at the Rainbird residence and Lacey had left the table early to retire to her room with her poodle. There she sat at her window until she saw Sir Roland come up the drive. With a sigh she went to her door and stopped. She couldn't go to him—not then. She wanted to tell him...and couldn't. The net result was that she got very little sleep and after dozing only a short while toward the early-morning hours, she awoke heavy-eyed and pale.

She dressed with little care, chirped to Peewee and proceeded outdoors to give her dog a run.

She was not the only one who did not sleep well. Sir Roland came down the stairs just as the front door closed at Lace's back. He wanted to follow her out but held himself in check. What was the good? Where was the sense in that? It would only lead to new torture. How could he look into her eyes...be so near and not touch her?

The viscount too had spent a restless night. He descended the stairs to find Sir Roland staring at the front door.

"Eh, old boy...you up too?"

Sir Roland smiled ruefully. "I've made an ill bed, my friend, and it is not at all comfortable."

Buzz sighed, "I'm not doing much better..." He thought of Flora. More and more, Lace's idealism made sense to him. More and more, he found it difficult to accept the values he had been brought up to believe in. Social standing? What did it mean in the end? "Did you see who went out, Ro? Was it Lace?"

"Yes . . . why?"

"Want to talk to her . . ." said Buzz, going toward the door.

"Oh? What about?" asked Roland more than curious, almost demanding.

The viscount put up a brow. "Personal . . . it's something very personal." With which he left his friend to stare after him.

"Confound it all!" snapped Sir Roland as the door closed before his eyes. He was helpless, totally helpless, gagged by his own hands, bound by his own means!

The viscount caught sight of Lace up ahead on the drive heading for the thicket. Peewee was bounding about in high spirits, barking and thoroughly enjoying himself as he chased every living thing in sight.

"Lace . . . hold . . . Lace . . ." called the viscount.

She turned and waited for his approach. "Yes, Buzz." There was no lilt to her voice and her eyes seemed drowned in sorrow.

"Good lord, girl . . . whatever is the matter? You look terrible!"

She smiled at that. "Do I? But that is not what you chased me down to say."

"No . . . I wanted to tell you . . . wanted to explain . . . about yesterday, about the things I said. They must have sounded terribly callous . . ."

"Worse."

"I know . . . and I won't try to excuse myself. I am not all wrong, my dear. You must understand that we cannot change society . . . try as we might, they will have their prejudices . . . and Miss Morely's unfortunate circumstances have put her on the outer rim of the society in which you and I live."

"But..."

"However, that does not mean that I would give her up if I loved her..."

"And do you? Love her, I mean?"

"Lace...Lace...how can I? I don't know her."

"Yet when you look at her you get a silly look on your face," noted Lace unmercifully.

He grinned. "Do I? Well, she is a lovely woman...soft...gentle..."

"How do you know...if you don't know her?" teased Lace.

"That much I know...one would realize it after being in her company only a moment...but I am rattling on to no purpose and that is not what I meant to do."

"No, you meant to improve my opinion of you as it now stands. You have not accomplished that, Buzz."

"Have I not? Why is that, Lace?"

"Because you have only sugar-coated what you have said yesterday afternoon. You would have courted Miss Morely...had she a dowry, had she not been Lady Stanhope's hired companion...you would have...admit it, Buzz!"

The viscount stopped and looked at her full. "Yes, perhaps..."

"Then how can I change what I think of you and your set of values?" retorted Lace uncompromisingly.

"Because the reasons I have given you are valid..."

"For whom? For what? To what end? Will you take some fine female of excellent background to be your wife? Will you...knowing it is Flora Morely that

193

occupies your thoughts? Oh...all of you are calculat
ing beasts!" She walked away from him. There was
nothing left for her to do but to confess her all to Sir
Roland and return home. Love? It was a fantasy, it
was unattainable. Tonight! She would tell Sir Roland
everything tonight...and in the morning she would
prepare to go home to her stepmother and face her
own reality!

He watched her head for the stables and called out
to her; she stopped and waited. "Lace...where are
you going...?"

"I thought I would pay Flora a morning call. Do
you wish to join me?" Peewee was yapping at her feet
and she stooped to pick him up.

"No...I don't think I had better..." he said
quietly.

"Fool!" she said and turned again.

"All right, then!" he retorted somewhat heatedly,
for his patience with her intolerance was at an end.
"I'll come...but I don't know what you hope to prove
by this!"

"Don't you?" She wanted to say more, but she had
gained this much and wasn't about to spoil it now.
She put Peewee into the hands of one of the livery
boys and asked him to take charge of the poodle until
her return. Some few minutes later they were driving
over to the Stanhope Estate in the viscount's open
and fashionable phaeton.

Uproarious conditions prevailed at the Stanhope
Estate. Servants went to and fro with smelling salts,
madeira, hot tea and timid words of encouragement
while her ladyship bewailed the fate of her diamonds
and vacillated between screeching and fainting fits.

It was Collymore who came in from an early-
morning ride to discover the disturbed state of affairs

and take over command. A lackey was dispatched to fetch Mr. Jacot, his aunt was made comfortable upon the parlor sofa and Miss Morely was left to attend her while Collymore went to question the servants.

However, order did not return in any degree until the appearance of Mr. Jacot, who came into the parlor quietly and yet most authoritatively. "Good-day to ye, m'lady...now don't be fretting, 'tis a rare set-to we 'ave 'ere but I thinks our lad has finally tripped himself up! Aye, I think he took on too much when he set himself to nabbing yer famous diamonds!"

"Oh, Mr. Jacot...do you think they may yet be recovered? They have been in my late husband's family for over a century...I can't bear to think they are really lost to the name..."

He patted her hand. "There, there, m'lady...we'll see...we'll see. If ye don't mind...I'd like to 'ave a look aboot the place...before I question yer people."

"Question my people...you mean my servants?" she asked with some horror.

"Lord love ye, madam...of course...and your nephew here as well..."

"Whatever do you mean by that?" ejaculated Collymore taken aback. "What can *I* tell you?"

"One never knows...but we'll see...in good time..." He left them to stare at one another.

It was at this point that Miss Lacey Eden and the Viscount Bussingham were announced. Lace and Buzz had already been informed by the harassed butler what was toward, so they came in on the scene with ready sympathy.

"My lady...how dreadful this is for you..." offered Lacey, dropping her a quick curtsy.

"You cannot imagine, my dear. My head quite aches...oh, how can I bear it, how can I?"

"I am certain this man Jacot will soon get to the bottom of this," offered the viscount, giving her ladyship's hand a perfunctory kiss. "I understand that the man is already investigating the grounds..."

"For what, confound him?" put in Collymore. "The man is a slow top...a country bumpkin...what can he hope to find by examining the park...?"

"Footprints in the garden beds beneath the window," offered Jacot, re-entering at that moment. "Oddly enough...there were none."

"Which means what?" demanded Collymore impatiently.

"Ah...it has its meaning. Now...if you please, m'lord...did you notice anything irregular last evening...?"

"How do you know the diamonds were stolen last evening...?"

"Her ladyship's maid tells me that she added an emerald ring to the collection in the drawer yesterday afternoon...and saw that the entire set was present at that time," returned Jacot quietly. "Now...if you will answer me question..."

"Irregular...no...not that I can think of...damn it, man, I don't know!" answered Collymore.

"I see..." mused Mr. Jacot to himself. He was now only stalling for time to elapse. His beadles were in the servants' quarters secretly searching the rooms and he was awaiting the results of that search.

"Well...what are you going to do now?" demanded Collymore.

He ignored the question and turned instead to Flora, who was sitting very close to Lace. She had been made nervous by the proceedings and she was twisting a handkerchief between her fingers. "Miss Morely...I find it most interesting that you were resent during those notorious London robberies as well as the two we have now had in our district..."

"I resent that!" snapped the viscount, jumping to is feet. "Everyone present was at the Rainbird state during *that* robbery...and any number of eople, including myself, were milling about during nose London crimes!"

"Aye, nobbut said different, m'lord...but, Miss Iorely now has one up on ye..." returned Jacot.

"Does she? What of Collymore?" cried the viscount isibly outraged.

Jacot turned to Collymore. "Aye...it would seem nat both Miss Morely and Lord Collymore have one oincidence too many."

The door burst open at that point prohibiting irther comment, for in its fold stood a very excited oung uniformed man. From his fingers he waved an merald ring. "Mr. Jacot...Mr. Jacot...lookee what ve found!"

All eyes discovered the prize the young beadle held nd her ladyship gasped. Mr. Jacot moved forward to ake it up. "Where did you find this, Mr. Henry?"

"In the chambers of one Miss Flora Morely!" nnounced the man portentiously.

Mr. Jacot was the only member of the assembled arty that did not turn 'round to stare at the poor girl. Ie fingered instead the ring very thoughtfully before resenting it to her ladyship and asking quietly, "Is his one of the missing pieces, m'lady?"

She nodded, for all speech was centered now in one hing—accusing Flora Morely. She gathered her gitation while Mr. Jacot turned to Flora. "Can ye xplain, lass?"

"Explain?" cried Flora in some confusion. 'No...how can I?"

"How indeed!" expostulated her ladyship, "*Thief!* I

have nurtured a viper in my home! Vile creature...
took you to me as I would my own blood..."

"Jest a moment there, m'lady..." put in Mr. Jacot
"No one is accusing Miss Morely of anything."

"But you have the evidence...?"

"Aye...that was a might convenient, wouldn't y
say? No...but I ain't saying she didn't have no par
in this...jest not saying she did. I believe in bein
careful aboot sech things."

"You say what you will, Mr. Jacot...but I shan'
have her in my house another moment!"

The tears were running freely down Flora'
cheeks. All this while Lace was stunned, too stunne
to say a word, but she came to life at this. Her arn
went about Flora's shoulders. "Come along, love. W
are going home." She turned to her ladyship. "Kindl
have Miss Morely's belongings delivered to th
Bussingham Estate, my lady."

"You cannot mean to take her to your mother'
home...not after what you know!" cried Lad
Stanhope to the viscount.

He was furious. His hands itched at his sides. Hov
dare she malign his Flora. His sweet, his inno
cent...his...but there wasn't time to analyze hi
feelings. "Know? What we know of Miss Morely i
that she is not capable of such a crime," snapped th
viscount as he took up Flora's arm.

She leaned heavily onto her good leg for her knee
felt weak, and his arm went immediately, support
ively around her waist.

"There, there, love...don't listen to any o
this...we'll have you home and safe in a brace o
snaps," said the viscount soothingly into her ear.

Jacot coughed into his round hand. "Er...ye mus
be remembering noa...well...Miss Morely ain't fre
to leave the district. She goes wit ye instead o

198

...but, lad, ye be responsible for her where-boots."

"I understand, Mr. Jacot." He turned to the company at large, "Good-day to you." Then he led Miss Morely out of the room.

Lace was frowning and as she passed Collymore he stopped. "Colly...tell me...if you had to point a finger at a servant in this house...who would it be?"

Collymore had been wondering about that very thing. He didn't for a minute think it was Flora Morely. In fact, his first thought was Stills. Why, he couldn't answer himself. He only knew that he had been trying to place the man's face for some time unsuccessfully.

"That wouldn't be quite fair, Lace...I have no fact to back up my own suspicions."

"But you have a suspicion...?"

"Yes...I don't like the man Stills..."

"He was helping at the Rainbird house the night of the ball—"

"Exactly so...but perhaps that is why he comes to mind."

"Thank you, Colly...You do believe Flora had nought to do with this?"

"I want to believe she had nought to do with it because *you* believe it..." he said softly.

"Precisely so, Colly..." She gave him a flirtatious look and then took her leave of Lady Stanhope. The viscount and Flora were awaiting the phaeton outdoors and she joined them just as a groom brought up the carriage.

With Flora neatly situated between the viscount and Lace they started off in silence, but this was soon broken. In spite of the warmth of the day Flora was shivering and Lace pulled up the blanket to place it over her friend's lap.

"Lace...Lace...how do you suppose...?"

"The ring? It was planted there, make no mistake Jacot thinks so as well or he would never have let you go. It was far too convenient...why would that one piece alone turn up? A pretty diversion, nothing else," she sighed. "What remains now is to get proof against our man?"

"Proof...we don't even know who our man is?" said the viscount.

"But we have our suspicions...for my part..." started Lace.

"Not Collymore...he is capable of many things...but I doubt..."

"No, silly, not Colly...and I have logic to support that belief. There is a man in Lady Stanhope's house who was at the Rainbird ball...he is a servant..."

"Stills!" cried Flora. "Of course...oh, my God.... have never liked him...and yesterday...I came upon him behind the stables. He was dallying with Bess...her ladyship's maid..."

"That explains how he knew where the diamonds were hidden!" cried Lace excitedly.

"Yes, but what has he done with the gems?" asked the viscount.

"I am not a crystal ball, Buzz...if I knew that would know who his accomplice is," she returned ruefully.

"So then we are certain he has an accomplice?" asked the viscount.

"Of course...Stills is no man to be planning such crimes. We have to keep in mind that he has been involved in those three London robberies as well...No, Stills may be quick of finger but not of mind. Let us suppose that when Flora walked into the Rainbird library Stills had already taken the goblets from their place...he was about to lower them out the window, in pops Flora...he hides behind the drapes...in comes Colly. Out goes Flora...out goes Colly...he drops the goblets out the window. Later...someone...perhaps a guest at the ball...retrieves the prize before Jacot arrives," summed Lace.

"It could have been Collymore..." said the viscount thoughtfully. "He could have been the accomplice."

"No...he escorted the dowager home. By the time he would have been able to return for the goblets...Jacot would have been there, and Jacot examined the ground beneath the windows and there was nothing there. No...Colly is not the accomplice."

"Shouldn't we go back and tell Mr. Jacot...about Stills..." cried Flora.

"No. I have a strong notion Jacot is far more needle-witted than any of us. He has Stills in mind...What I want to do is trap Stills into giving away his partner...which means we shall have to keep tabs on his comings and goings."

"I don't think he will meet with the partner now...not after this..."

"There is always the chance, and I am afraid that is all we can do."

Flora brushed away a tear. "I am so ashamed...going to Lady Bussingham...in this manner..."

"No, my dear. You could never have anything to be ashamed about."

"But Lady Stanhope will go about saying such dreadful things about me..."

"Will she? I think not...unless, of course, she wishes to be faced with a slander suit!" said the viscount on a hard note.

She looked up at him worshipfully. "You would...do that...?"

"And more...so much more..." he answered quietly.

Chapter Nineteen

LACEY MOVED PURPOSELY toward the library. Sir Roland was within, and she had made up her mind to it. She would wait no longer! Flora was napping above stairs and Lace was well satisfied with Jana Bussingham's behavior toward the girl, so there was nothing more to do but pay the piper!

She opened the door and stopped, for he stood by the fireplace, his elbow resting against the mantle, his thumb pressed to his lips and his face drawn in a hard line.

She closed the door quietly at her back and he turned. His eyes lit up and then his lashes shaded all their expression.

"Lace...is everything all right? Is Miss Morely resting?"

"She is fine ... but everything is not all right ... Sir Roland, you will in all probability despise me but I must tell you something ... show you something ..." She went to the desk drawer, opened it and withdrew the documents Mr. Farnsborough had left behind for Sir Roland's signature. Resolutely she walked to Sir Roland and placed them in his hand. "Read these."

He frowned but did what she asked. She could see the line of his brows, the furrow of his surprise etched on his countenance.

"What does this mean ...? How long have these papers been here?"

"Some days now ... and before you asked Letty to be your wife. They mean ... quite obviously, that you are now a financially independent man."

"Good God ... but ... why wasn't I told?"

"Foolishly ... I believed I could make you love me ... want me, in spite of your mercenary intentions toward Miss Rainbird. I didn't realize you were about to ... that you would ask her so quickly ... I thought ..."

"You let me propose to Letty ... knowing that I need not?" He was furious.

She could see the red darts of light in his eyes and knew well the extent of his wrath. "Please, Sir Roland ... I didn't know you would propose to her that night ... I would have told you ... was about to ..."

"About to?" he retorted angrily. "Yet you let it go on afterward without informing me! You have made a botch of it, haven't you?"

"Roland ... please ..." She daren't even tell him now about her real name or that she was an heiress herself. "Try and understand ... I wanted so for you to love me freely ... I wanted so ..."

"You wanted a fairy tale and ended by creating a

hell! Do you realize there is no way I can bow out of this marriage now? Do you?"

"I have been racking my mind trying to think of a solution. I was hoping to find one before I had to confess to you..."

"But finding none, you have decided to dump the muddle in my lap! Very fine work. Very fine work indeed!" He took up her shoulders and drew her to him. "Lace...Lace...don't you realize what your mistrust of me has done to our future?"

"Mistrust of you? How could I trust you? You were by your own admittance a fortune hunter. I wanted you to ask me to be your wife out of love for me...not because of money..."

"But why keep it from me...that I had inherited? Could I not be wealthy and love you as well?"

"Oh...I don't know...I don't know...it seemed the thing to do at the time and I was so sure...oh, bother! I had some silly, I suppose, quite childish notion at the time...but it didn't prove itself out and now what are we to do?"

"Are you at last putting up your hands? Are you finally asking me to involve myself in my own affairs?" he asked on a sardonic note. "Do you think I am truly capable of running my own life?"

"Don't be nasty to me, Roland...I couldn't bear it if you were to end in hating me..."

"Hate you?" he returned incredulously. "Don't you realize...can't you see how much I adore you?" With which he proceeded to display this very well.

At length he released her. "But this gets us nowhere...Lace, my own darling brat...I am pledged to marry Letty...however can I withdraw that pledge?"

"I don't perceive a solution myself...that is why I have confessed," she answered at once.

In spite of his agitation over the problem he let go a whoop of laughter. "Don't you, my little love? Nor do I? At least not at the moment."

"It is a good thing Mrs. Rainbird's mourning has prohibited a formal announcement going into the papers..."

"My dear love...what good is that when Mr. Rainbird made an announcement at the ball. It is no secret that Letty and I are bethrothed."

"Drat! We must think of something..."

At that moment the library doors opened and the butler appeared with a silver tray, which he offered to Lace. She glanced with some surprise at the envelope resting upon the silver before taking it up. "Thank you," she said quietly, dismissing him with her eyes.

She waited only long enough for the butler to close the door at his back before turning to look at Roland. "Now...who would be sending me this?"

Roland grinned. "Why don't you open it, love, and find out?"

"Yes, of course...it is just that...there is something about this that gives me the chills?"

He frowned. "Would you like me to open it?"

"No...I am being a whopstraw over nothing." She slit the envelope open with her finger, unfolded the paper and raised a curved brow over the contents.

Dearest love:
How can I leave in the morning without seeing you one last time. Without making one last attempt to win your heart? There is so much I have to tell you, words I have never before said.

I know too that you are deeply troubled by Miss Morely's problems. Rumor has it that she will soon be arrested. I have some information that you might be able to put to some good use.

Please...meet me tonight at nine o'clock at my balloon sight.

Forever yours,
Charles

She read it through twice and then exclaimed, "Ha! Whatever can he mean by such a ridiculous thing?"

Roland leaned forward and took it up from her. "May I?"

"Of course. It will do you good to see how many men want me," she bantered.

He read it, frowned darkly, but the tone of his voice belied the fierceness of his expression. "So, my brat, it would seem you go about the country making conquests of every man you meet!"

"Stuff! He doesn't love me...in fact, I have every good reason to believe that he has been dallying after *your* Letty!"

"What? Doing it up brown?"

"Why would I?"

"I have yet to fathom the workings of your mind." He was grinning, putting both arms around her.

"Ho, there, you miserable rake, you are still a promised man!" She was only teasing but it sobered him and he stiffened. She pinched at his arm. "But not for long, my love...at least not to Letty."

"But to get back to Letty...what makes you think Mr. Teggs was pursuing her?"

"They knew each other in London, I think...and she has been meeting him at his balloon sight...I have long thought they had rather a thing for one another...but hold a moment...I have just had a notion!" Suddenly the answer to their problem presented itself. Roland would never approve, so she must keep it from him until it was done.

She pulled herself away from his touch. "I must go...I just remembered an errand I must discharge at once!"

He watched her with some misgiving, for she took the note from Charles Teggs with her. "Lace..." he called to her. "I think we had better discuss this errand of yours..."

"No...oh, no...for then you would be honor-bound to stop me and I shall brook no interference, Roland my love."

"You shall brook no..." But she was already out of sight. His lady was totally incorrigible and totally captivating, but this time he meant to keep a close eye on her doings. She had had free reign long enough.

Lace hastened to her room where she resealed Charles Teggs's letter. She then went to the stables and put it in one of the hands of the grooms advising him that it should go to Letty Rainbird without delay and that no one was to know it came with a Bussingham servant. She placed a coin for himself and a coin for the servant at the Rainbird residence in his pockets and watched him ride off on one of the Bussingham nags. This done there was nothing left but to wait for evening, when she would have to call upon the viscount for help!

Collymore watched the increasing darkness with something akin to intolerance. He was heartily sick of his aunt's moaning and groaning and wished desperately that she would take herself above stairs to her chambers so that he might be off to a night's pleasures. The moon was full, the stars bright and the sky a delight to gaze upon, but suddenly his contemplation of nature shifted to a dark, moving object. The object slinked, turned and the rays hit his face. Stills! What the devil...? And then he realized.

Stills was familiar because he had seen him in London...slinking away from the Winthrop ball...directly after the robbery! Stills! Why hadn't he realized sooner? There was just enough time to get outside and follow the man.

"Where are you going...Colly...?" cried her ladyship as she watched him dash for the doors.

"No time, madam...I will explain later!" he snapped as he dived out of the room.

At Bussingham, a lively argument was nearly reaching its peak, as each debator took a firm stand and would not budge.

Lacey was nearly ready to pull her hair out by its roots, so great was her agitation. She paced to and fro in the library until Roland could bear her distress no more. He moved to stand in front of her and took up her bare arms in his tight and yet exceedingly tender grasp. "Be still, Lace..."

"How can I? *You* won't cooperate...Buzz proses on and on...don't you realize that unless you go along with my scheme all will be lost...and besides...there is no saying that Letty may be in danger..."

"Letty in danger? Whatever do you mean?" exclaimed Jana Bussingham.

"You see...I know that she is going to meet Charles Teggs at his balloon sight...because I sent that note...you know, Roland...the one I received today...I sent it to her."

"Devil a bit!" expostulated her beloved. "Will you never cease to plunge yourself into one scrape after another?"

"I don't understand..." said Lady Bussingham.

"Nor I," agreed her son.

"It doesn't matter that you don't understand," put

209

in Flora softly. "I think we should trust Lace in this...and just do what she asks."

"Thank you, Flora!" said Lace, her chin up.

"Yes, but you are quite out there, my sweet," said the viscount, patting Flora's hand. "You are not yet aware to what depths this rogue of ours can go."

"But I have already gone there...and now 'tis for you to rescue me!" declared Lacey in a tone near to shouting.

"Yes, then...let us say that we go along with your mode of thought, my brat...there is still no saying that Letty will meet him," said Roland allowing his hand to stroke her arm.

She dimpled up at him. "*She* will go...mark me...and if she doesn't...it will only mean that we shall have to find another way."

"But you are asking me to go to her parents...accuse the girl of not being at home..." answered Roland pointedly.

"Yes...and if she is at home, you will apologize, after all, 'tis not your fault that someone has misinformed you!"

"But, Lace...what note did you send her...? What makes you think she is meeting this Teggs tonight?" asked Lady Bussingham.

"I received a love letter of sorts...but it wasn't addressed to me...only to 'dearest love.' I know that Letty and Mr. Teggs held each other in some esteem...at least I suspected it, so I sent the note to Letty after resealing it. She will be curious enough about its contents to go to him...besides...I think she rather enjoys clandestine meetings, but that is only my own feeling in the matter. Now, what I want is for Roland to go to her home and rouse her father into searching her room...and then taking him to the balloon sight to observe his daughter with Mr. Teggs. *Voilà*... engagement is off!"

"'Tis sordid!" said the viscount in some disgust.

"But quite necessary," answered his mother. "After all... if the girl is with Mr. Teggs... I should rather think you would want your best friend freed from her."

The viscount found this bit of reasoning oddly logical and retreated to think it over, while once more Lace took command.

"Now, then... off with you Roland... and you, Buzz... you are coming with me."

"Where are we going?"

"To the balloon sight, of course."

"But... why... ?" he asked dumbfounded.

"I really don't know... perhaps I just want to see the fruition of my schemes and *you*, I am persuaded for all your talk, cannot be so pudding-hearted that you don't want to see what is going to happen?"

"As a matter of fact, that is probably the best notion that you have had yet. I do indeed wish to accompany you and make certain that this affair is not botched up any further!" snapped the viscount haughtily.

Lace laughed and took to shooing Sir Roland out of the house while pulling the viscount along with her. At the library doors, she turned to Flora and Lady Bussingham. "Wish me luck."

"The best of it, dear... and we shall be sitting on pins until you return with the close of this absurd adventure!" returned Lady Bussingham, patting Flora's hand reassuringly as Lace waved good-bye!

So it was that within a very short span of time Sir Roland dismounted from his horse and put it into the keeping of the Rainbird livery boys. He was shown into the library where he was soon joined by Mr. Rainbird, who came in with hand extended to receive his future son-in-law.

"But, sir...this is most unusual..." said Mr. Rainbird jovially. "A pleasure, I do assure you...I suppose you find it a hard thing to keep away from our Letty...eh?" He poked Roland in the ribs.

Roland decided to change his purpose. "Indeed...I was riding past on the way home and thought I might say good night to her."

"Indeed...indeed...she will be delighted!" with which he rang for a lackey, who was then dispatched after Miss Rainbird.

Several moments elapsed while the gentlemen in the parlor sipped their port when Mrs. Rainbird appeared in a somewhat agitated state. "It's Letty...oh, dear...dear...she is not in her room...she is nowhere in the house...where can she be? What can this mean?"

Mr. Rainbird heartily wished his wife at Jericho for such an outburst. Letty was given to waywardness now and again. He had thought when they left London that it was behind them. Apparently she was at it again, but this was not the time to go spouting it off in front of Sir Roland. "You must be mistaken..." he said in a low voice to his wife.

"No...I regret that I don't think she is mistaken. I must confess to you, Mr. Rainbird...that I rather thought I saw Letty riding off across the field...believing myself in error I continued on my way here," put in Roland quietly.

"Riding across the fields...but to where?" ejaculated Mr. Rainbird.

"It has recently come to my attention that your

aughter has a very close friendship with Mr.
eggs..." he suggested.

"The balloonist!" shouted Mr. Rainbird.

"Oh...no...no...I thought she had done with
at terrible man," cried Mrs. Rainbird.

"I believe, sir...that I know where they may be at
is very moment, if you will but accompany me,"
aid Roland authoritatively.

"Accompany you? Confound the devil! He will
ish himself in hell when I get through with him,"
aid Mr. Rainbird, making for his doors and calling
r his hat and greatcoat.

Sir Roland contained himself and followed suit. In
king Lacey to his heart, he had taken on a storm.
e could foresee a future filled with preposterous
rapes and he looked with relish to each and every
ae his brat would hand him!

Chapter Twenty

COLLYMORE LEANED INTO a tree and drew a long breath. It was hard work keeping up with the shifty man ahead. Damn the fellow, he wasn't going to get away with those diamonds! When he inherited from his aunt he wanted his estate intact.

Stills felt a chill creep up his spine and he stopped to have himself a look, but he could see no one at his back. He wasn't supposed to be going out to meet Charles Teggs tonight and he rather hoped this little surprise visit to the balloon site would prove a waste of time. He liked the business relationship he had with the flash cove, but something told him that Charles Teggs was finally giving in to his greed. Well, the flash wasn't taking off in any balloon so long as he was alive to stop him!

Lacey and Buzz tethered their horses a good distance from the balloon site and walked at a steady and somewhat stealthy pace through the thicket to a position that would allow them ample visibility. From where they crouched they could see Mr. Teggs working the rigging of his balloon and the entire thing made Lace feel that the man was ready to ascend at any moment. She watched, her lips pursed until a dark female form on a horse came into view. Charles Teggs smiled and went to greet her.

"Darling..." he started and then stopped short. "Letty..."

She put her hands upon his shoulders and allowed him to lift her down from her mount. Her arms went 'round him and she pulled him hotly to her embrace.

-He was in no mood. He didn't understand her presence here. He was worried lest Lace arrive and find him with Letty. He had to get her away. "Letty...you shouldn't be here..." he said moving backward, frowning disapprovingly.

"I...I...what are you talking about? You sent me a note...this note," she said, pulling the folded paper out of her gloved hand.

He took it, unfolded it and perused it long enough to discover it was the letter he had intended for Lace. "This...this is impossible..." he said in a half whisper.

"But it is your handwriting. Did you not mean for me to receive it?" asked Letty in some bewilderment.

He had a problem on his hands. He had intended to lure Lace here tonight and to take her up in his balloon. He would then keep her in his protection while he blackmailed her family. That had all gone awry...but here was Letty...and the same thing could be done, however...he cared for Letty...in his

216

fashion and it was a more difficult thing for him to do with her as the victim.

"Let me think..." he said, putting his fist to his tight mouth.

"But Charles...I don't understand any of this. You send me a note with some nonsense about Flora Morely...whom I don't give two groats for...and you say to meet you...then when I do, you don't seem to want me..."

He turned on her sharply. "Not want you? I have wanted you from the start! What if I told you I lured you out here with every intention of taking you away with me by force?"

"I would not go!" She stamped her foot. "You would never do that..."

He grabbed hold of her arm. "Would I not? You have teased me, my love, once too often. I want you..."

"It is my money you want..." she pouted, but as he pulled her into his arms and took her chin in his hand she melted to his kiss, and it was sweetly passionate.

He set her away a moment. "Yes, my Letty...I need your money and all it can do for us...but, never fear, I need you as well."

"But I don't wish to be your wife...it would not hold the respectability being married to Sir Roland holds..."

"You are in your own way a mercenary jade, my love..." He broke off as a dark figure loomed before him in the distance and he waited until the figure took on shape and form with proximity.

"Stills! What the deuce are you doing here?"

"Aye...I might be asking ye the same," said Stills none too sweetly.

Teggs was quick. "You can see why I am

here...and we don't need company."

"Don't ye...but now...as it happens ye may be wanting someone to look after yer balloon there...seeing as it's all fine and ready."

"Who is this man? What does he want?" cried Letty in some fear.

"Never mind him...look Stills..."

"Ye got greedy, didn't ye, Flash...I could cut ye in two...but I'll stall meself and settle fer taking me fair share of the sparklers..."

"Stills...be reasonable...you wouldn't know where to sell them and get a fair price..."

"Sparklers? Sell them...what are you talking about?" Letty was visibly shaken by this discussion, for she was beginning to see, all too clearly.

In the thicket the viscount stiffened and Lacey held his arm.

"Did you not think as much...?" she said. "I did...or at least I wondered."

"Of course...what fools we have been not to realize...and Lace, he must have the jewels on him if he intended to take off in his balloon."

"On him...or in the basket of the balloon..." she suggested. "Now if only Roland will get here before Jacot makes his move."

"Jacot...?"

"I sent him a note earlier this afternoon...regarding Stills and my suspicions about Teggs. You see, after discussing the matter with your mother, we settled it between us that Teggs was at each and every London house that was robbed..." But she cut herself off as Sir Roland and Mr. Rainbird rode up and Mr. Rainbird was none too quiet about his arrival.

"Letty! Get over here, child ... behind me! We shall discuss your behavior later after I finish with this swine!"

Letty began to wail, "Sir Roland ... oh ... you must not think ..."

"I am afraid, Letty, that I can think only one thing," he said gravely.

"But he is nothing to me ..."

"Yet you are here with him ..." He turned to Mr. Rainbird. "Mr. Rainbird, I dislike putting you to further upset, but I should like you to know that I feel I can no longer serve Miss Rainbird as I might have done."

"You wish to withdraw from the engagement?"

"I feel it is the only honorable thing to do."

"Of course ... some excuse will be made ..." He turned to Teggs. "And *you* ... scoundrel ... stay ... where do you think you are going?"

During the interim Teggs and Stills had been inching toward the balloon. Stills had succeeded in dislodging two out of the three pegs that held the ropes to earth.

It was at this point that Collymore appeared from behind the balloon and just in time to block Teggs from jumping into the basket. He grappled with the man while Sir Roland gave chase to Stills.

The viscount jumped to his feet and ran into the fracas ready to lend his fives should they be needed, while Lace ran to Mr. and Miss Rainbird. Letty's mouth opened and closed and then she looked at Lace. "*You* ... what are you doing here? What is going on?"

Lace did not have the opportunity to answer, for she saw the flash of a knife and ran forward screaming to Sir Roland, "Ro ... he has a knife ... Ro ...!"

Sir Roland saw this, dodged it, cracked his hand sharply over the man's wrist, doubled his fists, and brought them roughly onto Stills's head. It was at this point that Jacot arrived on the scene with two beadles.

Collymore and Roland were relieved of their nefarious charges and came breathing hard into the circle that had formed.

"I think, Jacot... you will find the jewels somewhere in the lining of the basket..." offered the viscount, wishing he had had more to do with all of this.

Roland's arm went around Lacey reassuringly as she seemed bent on examining every inch of him for injuries. Collymore glanced their way and objected, "I say... Buzz... don't you think you should be protecting Lace from Roland's advances... I mean... he is a promised man!"

"No longer... at least... not to Miss Rainbird..." He turned to Lace and lifted her chin. "... which reminds me... I never did get around to proposing to you, Miss Eden..."

"Oh... Ro... that brings me to one other confession..."

"May heaven spare me. What is it?"

"I am not Miss Eden."

"You are, of course, some lowly creature with no stepmother, no background whatsoever, whom I am very certain I shall go through life adoring whatever her name may be."

"That was very prettily said, Ro... but I fear I must tell you, my name is Lace... Burton... and I am quite rich, you know... terribly so."

"Burton... *you* are the Burton heiress?" he demanded.

She nodded shamefacedly. "So you see how very

wicked I have been ... but I did so want you to love me before you knew."

"Hold!" cried Collymore. "You cannot give yourself to him, he is nought but a fortune hunter!"

"Ex-fortune hunter," returned Lace happily. "He has inherited, you see, which makes it all quite comfortable."

Letty let go a long wail and all attention turned her way. Collymore was grumbling and Lacey was hit with another idea. She put a quick kiss to Sir Roland's lips and inched toward Collymore. "Colly ... Letty will need a groom if she is to weather the talk that will spring up from her broken engagement."

"I suppose ... but what has that to do ..." He stopped short.

"Precisely so." She let go a sigh. "Now, Buzz ... Ro ... I suggest we go home, for Aunt Jana and Flora are waiting for us!"

Buzz looked up from where he stood beside Jacot. "You two go on, I think I'll just stay awhile and see what they uncover here ..."

Roland took his love's arm and led her to Cricket and then, using the horse as a shield from observing eyes, said, "My own true love ... before we embark upon this life together ... is there anything else you would like to confess?"

"Only what you already must realize ... how very much I love you, Sir Roland Keyes ... from the very moment of our meeting."

"Lovely liar! Romantic goose. You could not have loved me right away ..."

"Well, perhaps not from the very first moment, but very soon afterward ... I think when you offered up your handkerchief for Peewee's puddle." She giggled. "And you ... when did you know you loved me?"

"I don't know, really...it came upon me slowly, insidiously, creepingly..."

"Stop! You make it sound a veritable plague."

"A delicious one. Now kiss me, brat!"

Very unlike herself she became quite pliable as she surrendered to his command.

By the year 2000, 2 out of 3 Americans could be illiterate.

It's true.

Today, 75 million adults...about one American in three, can't read adequately. And by the year 2000, U.S. News & World Report envisions an America with a literacy rate of only 30%.

Before that America comes to be, you can stop it...by joining the fight against illiteracy today.

Call the Coalition for Literacy at toll-free **1-800-228-8813** and volunteer.

**Volunteer
Against Illiteracy.
The only degree you need
is a degree of caring.**

Ad Council   Coalition for Literacy

LV-2

THIS AD PRODUCED BY MARTIN LITHOGRAPHERS
A MARTIN COMMUNICATIONS COMPANY